PRAISE FOR THORNTON PARSONS

Go Tell Aunt Rhody

"A REAL PAGE TURNER! The author has found a unique voice to tell the story of a woman in the present who is embroiled in the past. Ms. Parsons uses a casually breezy and folksy style to tell an intriguing tale. I eagerly await Thornton Parsons's second novel!"

– E. Meeks "quikwit1" (Chattanooga, TN), ***Amazon Reviews***

"VERY WELL-WRITTEN. Hard to put down. Ms. Parsons makes you feel that you know the characters and what they are feeling. I didn't want it to end. I wanted more. It will make a great movie."

– Radar-Ziva, *Amazon Reviews*

"GREAT BOOK! Just delicious! You will get drawn in by the characters. Very hard to put down! Has a very lovely ending."

– LilBlondeHairGirl, *Amazon Reviews*

"FIVE STARS. I have just finished reading Go Tell Aunt Rhody and loved the read. From the first chapter you are drawn into the characters and look forward to the next chance to continue reading. The main characters have great depth and feel like a friend that is sharing a mystery with you. The vehicle for setting up the plot is well thought out and believable. The story has enough twists and unexpected turns to keep the mystery buff content for hours. The librarian's rational to compare books to the personality of people is so well done that I will always remember those lines. This is a definite 'buy this book' alert."

– Book Worm, Columbia, Ky USA, *Amazon Reviews*

"**WELL-DONE INDEED!** *Go Tell Aunt Rhody* has two stories, one in the past, one in the present, both involving women, one of whom, Cathy, is fascinated when she finds the years' past diary of Lynette, a woman from the 1930s. In addition to everyday happenings, the diary contains a tale of infidelity and murder... Characterization here is excellent and the pace is good and fast despite the necessarily repetitive language in the diary entries. When the diary ends abruptly, Cathy can not rest until she learns what happened next. Neither could I!"

– Arline Chase, author of *Killraven, Ghost Dancer,* and the Spirit series, *Spirit of Earth, Spirit of Fire*, etc.

Go Tell Aunt Rhody

by Thornton Parsons

Cambridge Books
an imprint of
WriteWords, Inc.
Cambridge, MD 21613

Print Edition, February, 2013

Publisher's Note: This is a work of fiction. All characters and events portrayed in this book are fictional, and any resemblance to real people or incidents is purely coincidental.

Cambridge Books is a subsidiary of:

Write Words, Inc.
2934 Old Route 50
Cambridge, MD 21613

ISBN 978-1-61386-088-5

Fax: 410-221-7510

Bowker Standard Address Number: 254-0304

Dedication

This book is dedicated to my mother, Beverly Lake, who, during my childhood in Portland, Oregon, recognized my literary potential and that I was destined to write. Had she lived, it is my belief, that she would be very proud.

Go tell Aunt Rhody
Go tell Aunt Rhody
Go tell Aunt Rhody,
The old gray goose is dead.

She died in the millpond,
Died in the millpond,
Died in the millpond,
Standing on her head.

The one she'd been saving,
The one she'd been saving,
The one she'd been saving,
To make a feather bed.

The goslings are crying,
The goslings are crying,
The goslings are crying,
Because their mother's dead.

The gander is weeping,
The gander is weeping,
The gander is weeping,
Because his wife is dead.

Go tell Aunt Rhody,
Go tell Aunt Rhody,
Go tell Aunt Rhody,
The old gray goose is dead.

—Unknown

Chapter 1

"Died in the millpond, died in the millpond, died in the millpond," echoed the eerie strains through the darkness of a cavernous wooden structure. Cathy raised up to see, in the light of the kerosene lamp, two silhouettes arguing in earnest. The larger of the two paced around what seemed to be a concrete floor strewn with hay, kicking against an iron rail at selected intervals; each kick a resounding thud. The other sat on a crate across from the rail, hunched over, crying uncontrollably.

Cathy slid her feet from under the covers and over the side of the bed, but could not find the floor. Suddenly the pacing figure ran to what appeared to be a stall, or tool room, and retrieved an axe. A high-pitched wail came from the woman sitting on the crate, as the axe came crashing down through the darkness, splattering blood across Cathy's face. Lost in a black void, Cathy had fallen backwards onto her bed, unable to see more, but able to hear the clanging of metal against metal.

Gripped with fear, she pulled her legs back up and under the covers, unable to speak. Suddenly, the cold heartless moon seemed to drift from behind darkened clouds, and its light shimmered on water. From her vantage point in her bed at the water's edge, she observed the water milfoil and yarrow, pulsating, rising and falling with the duckweed as tiny ripples undulated underneath before lapping the shore. Two silhouettes rowed silently to the middle of the water and as the darkened clouds returned to hide the nocturnal orb, Cathy could hear gurgling sounds amid muffled sobs.

* * *

An October sun, which had ineffectively attempted to penetrate the low cloud cover, suddenly met with measurable success as it streamed through the laced curtains of Cathy's bedroom window. *That nightmare again!* She lay in bed, her heart pounding and her body bathed in perspiration. Cathy pushed back her hair from her moist forehead and heaved great sighs of relief as she became oriented to her surroundings. In the light of day, the nightmare evaporated and she felt pressed to remember the details, but could not concentrate.

As the adrenaline rush subsided, she drew her sleeve across her eyes, still not ready to rise. Little did she know that the glorious orb of the day had awakened her, not only to a vibrantly colorful autumn Friday, but also to a glimpse of the past; forgotten lives from a more formidable, yet more civilized decade...and the specter of murder.

The remnants of the dream floated as wispy cobwebs in her head, and each time that she would grasp an image of a symbol, it fled hastily, just beyond her grasp, to the recesses of her subconscious. Her eloquent brown eyes, prone to grayish-green optics, clouded with vexation. She did not know how long she had slept, probably several hours, for the previous day had proved strenuous. Even though her head felt heavy and congested, she gradually roused to her surroundings. She felt no sudden urge to action; no pressing issues.

With a sigh of satisfaction, she stretched her body and relaxed on fluffy pillows, not wanting to leave the warmth and comfort of her bed. In the employ of Shepherd-of-the-Hills Nursing Home, Cathy found that every minute of her working day was filled with tedious, but meaningful, job performance involving the care given to the residents. Most of her days were spent in service to others, and her patient load was such that she rarely had a spare minute to herself; none of the nursing assistants did.

Shepherd-of-the-Hills did provide gainful employment: an hourly-paid position, when she would have preferred a salary. She had always had an affinity for older people, having been taught respect for her elders in her youth, and felt drawn to them. Perhaps, the curiosity of their age, as well as their experience with life drew her as a magnet seeks out steel; or maybe, she had been born at the wrong time, and should have actually been born several decades earlier, and could relate to people from what should have been her era, too. Somehow, she felt that these people *were* her people.

Cathy did not understand senility, the degenerative processes of old age that many times culminates in dementia, as her grandmother had called it. Now, Alzheimer's had a name, but its terrible, ugly face remained the same, generation after generation. Still, when some of her patients had their "good" days, she took advantage of these lucid moments to explore the past, hoping for a clue that might guide her to the answers to questions that had burned holes into her heart.

She had never, in her life, been fully able to confront herself; to understand why she felt the way she did about particular issues, and to truly know herself. A thirst for knowledge and wisdom propelled her to seek answers through religion, philosophy, and principles, each leaving her thirst unquenched. So, she looked to the source: those who had been there and experienced Existence, unfulfilled. Shepherd-of-the-Hills allowed her a search field, nonpareil, in that no two days were alike, that might yield a crumb or two of understanding on her own journey of self-discovery. On her off days, however, she enjoyed sleeping in peaceful solitude, undisturbed by call buzzers.

Cathy rolled onto her side and peered at her bedside clock. Not quite noon, she thought, making no effort to rise. Throughout the house, she could hear none of the weekday noises: water running, footsteps on the stairs, radios, and the arguing voices of her teenaged children as they readied themselves for school.

Michael, a tall, handsome high school senior, worked at his uncle's auto body shop and proved to be quite adept and meticulous in his work. Blue-eyed, blond-haired Heather, on the other hand, spent most of her time with her sophomore cheerleader friends, working in Team Corps, an after school cheerleader program for middle grade students. Team Corps did not hold the remuneration for Heather that the body shop did for Michael, but he did keep her car in running order and she would reciprocate by fixing up a date for him with one of her cheerleader friends.

Her offspring on their own schedules, Cathy found that the silence, a silence without interest, was deafening and finally decided to get out of bed. She considered herself to be sensible, with few whims, and found no impropriety in sleeping late on her off days, free from any guilt at not having risen to wait on her family.

Donned in blue jeans and a wooly brown cardigan, she ran a comb through her blond mass before making her way to the kitchen for coffee. She sat in a comfortable chair on the deck and leisurely sipped. *Harry will be home tonight.* Leaning her head back, she inhaled deeply from her cigarette, aware of the absence of stress. She was amazed at how blue the sky seemed in contrast to the vermilion and gold of the autumn leaves. *What a perfect day!*

Staring up into the Columbia blue, her vision followed a jet that was trailed by a flawless white stream. Suddenly, a Monarch butterfly fluttered into her field of vision. *The jet and the butterfly; the butterfly and the jet.* Optically illusionary, their paths seemed destined to collide, like taxis at an imaginary intersection, and Cathy watched and waited. It was not long before the Monarch flitted from the forefront as the jet continued on, one totally unaware of the other, and Cathy stared into the blue vastness, only noticing the butterfly and the jet, peripherally.

She stubbed her cigarette out in an ashtray and went inside for another cup of coffee. She placed the vanilla creamer in the refrigerator and made mental notes of what she could possibly prepare for Harry's dinner that evening. The highway was his home for three to four days of each week, as he drove a tractor and trailer, and on his off days, he did not care for eating his meals in restaurants.

Before he had left for the road, Harry had transformed their small garage into a workshop for Cathy, who possessed the propensity and vision for taking dilapidated furniture, refinishing and refurbishing, until the discarded item, renewed, was once again serviceable. At times, a certain piece would capture her attention, and she felt comfort being near it. She questioned that, perhaps at another time, she had been someone else, reincarnated, and had actually owned this particular piece of furniture. The answer usually eluded her, but the prospects gave her an inner peace.

Every now and then, she would find a buyer for a piece that she had restored, but she found that the money did not equal the energy and expertise that went into each and every endeavor. She had great difficulty letting go.

Still, the extra cash flow, as Michael called it, enabled her to scour flea markets and junk shops for another castoff treasure waiting to be reborn. Harry would also surprise her with items of interest that he had found during his travels, and this particular run had taken him to Florida. Traveling to his destination, in what seemed to be endless hours in his truck, fatigued him, and once he had rested, he looked forward to going out and searching for items for Cathy. These jaunts allowed him to leave the truck yards, and eased his boredom. On this run, Cathy hoped that he would have the time to hastily rummage through some local junk stores during his layover.

She missed Harry, but over the years had grown quite used to this routine. When her children were younger, her time was always filled; their school activities and general neediness keeping her occupied. As they had grown older, they had adapted to their independence much easier than Cathy had, as evidenced by their extracurricular activities and social events, and by Cathy's difficulty in letting go. Harry had returned home many times to referee a fight between his wife and his children. Even though he did not always side with Cathy, she knew, in her heart of hearts, that he was usually right. Absence from the family had instilled in him an acute understanding, as well as an objectivity that she could only possess if she were able to distance herself, too.

Now, Cathy felt no pressure when Harry was away and looked forward to the days when he was home. Today, however, she was filled with a causeless, unshakable optimism, and her feelings gave way to a rushed excitement teetering on the brink of discovery, yet she could not pinpoint the presentiment. Her sixth sense was awake, prompting her, but not to the extent that she understood.

For some reason, Cathy stood for long moments in front of the slider, sipping her coffee as she gazed out across the deck and back yard. Something was nagging at her, but she couldn't quiet her mind long enough to decide what it was. It felt to her to be a complete and inexplicable happiness; something expected. She opened the door and took her seat on the deck and lit another cigarette. It seemed that she was emerging from a dark forest and the opportunity to see new things, think new ideas, and to expand her horizons lay just before her.

As she savored her steamy cup, her attention was captive to the splendor of the southeastern autumn, fresh and mysterious, with all of its aromatic overtones that had burst through this day following what seemed to be, a dry and lengthy, endless summer. It held promise as it conquered the scorching days and muggy nights of the preceding weeks.

For most of the year, the deck was where she spent what she called her "golden hour." This was the first hour of her day that belonged to her and to no one else, and she would spend it relaxing, collecting her thoughts, and planning her day. In this quiet, still hour of her morning, she could meditate and listen more to Nature, and less of the world. In this self-accounting of solitude, she found that she could sift through her thoughts and ponder Life, itself. She felt secure in the knowledge that there were reliable laws of the Universe, that she knew on her soul level, enabled her to work and learn on a conscious level. Her best ideas had come to her through silence and understanding, and she did not know whether to attribute them to genius or inspiration, but she was inwardly appreciative, whatever the source.

A faint sibilant sound drew her gaze skyward past the treetops where she observed two buzzards floating on the air, dipping and circling. *An omen. One is for sorrow, two is for joy, three for a letter, four for a boy...hm, must be joy. I knew it!*

Strangely, she did not feel disturbed, unlike other afternoons when she would perform routine activities for her patients, sometimes working with slow, methodical measures; others working with feverish, haphazard energy. During the uneventful days, she would sit on the deck and think and smoke, feeling relief from all of the tension. She thought a lot about karma, and held in great esteem, the harmony and orderliness of the Universe.

Today was one of those days, however, her feeling more than just content. Her joy felt boundless, as when one is in anticipation of a journey or a vacation, or even a three-day weekend. The air of expectancy gave her heart a buoyant feeling, and she waited, not knowing what had prompted it. As she pondered this curious feeling, her thoughts began to flash, uncontrollably, at lightning speed, but no bells and whistles. She fought the chaos that was forming in her mind and consciously corralled her mustang imagination to the Billings' "ranch," as she referred to their home.

Harry and Cathy had planned their lives together and had bought their home before Michael and Heather had been born. For a time, it seemed that they would have no children, but Michael was born shortly before their eighth wedding anniversary. In the meantime, Cathy had worked outside her home while Harry was away, and when he was home, they would spend their time painting walls and remodeling rooms, planting flowers and shrubbery, and perfecting their domicile.

Shortly after Michael was born, Heather arrived and Cathy found herself with two babies, both in diapers, and not a spare minute to call her own. But, she never regretted it. Now, however, her children were a source of great pride and a security that comes from knowing that at the end of her life, she would never be alone. Harry seemed to always be alone, and he did not quite understand her feelings.

Then, it came to her. *Meatloaf! Harry's favorite.* As she sipped her coffee, a smile of quiet satisfaction came to her lips. *One more cup of coffee and then, off to the grocery store!*

Chapter 2

Harry Billings dropped his truck at the yard and drove home in his own vehicle, arriving shortly before seven. The chill of the Tennessee autumn evening brought a sense of relief that prompted Cathy to hide her elation that he had made it home once more. She had learned that it was futile to worry about Harry while he was on the road, but just the same, she genuinely thanked God that he had made it back home safely.

"Hey, you," Harry said, kissing Cathy gently, his plain, kind face breaking into a contented smile, "I've got a surprise for you. It's out in my pickup."

"What is it?" she inquired, glancing behind him.

"Later...what's for dinner?"

"Your favorite. What did you find, Harry?"

"Just another old piece of junk for you to work on. I found it down in Cedartown, Georgia. I'll go get it and put it in the garage."

"Good," she answered, smiling, "I'll get dinner on the table and have a look at it after we eat."

Cathy stood on her tiptoes to kiss his tanned face, which was marked only by a furrow on his brow. A slight paunch around his middle and his brown hair graying at the temples, framing his receding hairline, were the only telltale signs that he was reaching his middle years. She was grateful that Time had been good to Harry; he *had* aged gracefully. After twenty-seven years of marriage, she loved him as much as she did in high school.

She heard the garage door opening as she was setting the table, and suppressed the temptation to go out and assess the potential of her new project. Looking up from the table, Cathy noticed Heather coming through the door.

"Are you home for dinner?" Cathy queried.

"What are we having?" Heather asked in return, tossing her silky blond tresses over her shoulder.

"Meatloaf and...."

"Mom," Heather sounded exasperated, "That's red meat! You know I don't eat red meat."

"Your loss."

"That's okay. Angela and I are going to take Michael a plate at the shop before we go to the football game, so we'll just grab a salad. That's much healthier." She darted up the stairs to her room to ready herself for her night out.

Heather took pride in her appearance and dressed fashionably in her cheerleader uniform. Many of Cathy's family members had commented how much Heather looked like her mother when she was in high school, and Cathy beamed at the compliments. Heather's long, silken hair and fair complexion foretold that she was, indeed, a beautiful girl. Her slim figure and angelic face enhanced her popularity at school, while her generous and compassionate nature ensured it. Her rebellious nature was not such that Cathy could not trust her to go where she told her she was going, but, when it came to Heather, Cathy distrusted the world.

Her years in the medical field had shown her some of the worst that Life meted out, and that was another reason why she preferred the sanctuary of Shepherd-of-the-Hills.

"Heather!" Cathy called as her daughter started out the door.

"What is it? Hurry, Angela's waiting," came the curt reply.

"You call me if you're going to be late. Now, come here and give me some sugar."

Heather sighed impatiently and rolled her eyes. Muttering to herself, she rushed into the kitchen and stood behind Harry's chair, leaning in toward Cathy and half-hugging her as she kissed her cheek.

"I love you, Sweetheart," Cathy called, as Heather ran out the door.

"Love you, Daddy; love you, Mom!" Then, the door slammed behind her.

"Looks like she's in quite a hurry," Harry observed, as he entered the room.

"She always is."

Cathy nodded to Harry and inhaled deeply the rich smell of warm meatloaf, mashed potatoes, and green peas. Harry always showered and went to bed early on his first night home, and Cathy knew that this meal would be the sustenance she needed to toil late into the night while Harry slept. He washed his hands at the kitchen sink while Cathy brought the rolls to the table. While they sat together to dine, she looked deeply into his gentle hazel eyes and squeezed his hand, knowing that tomorrow night she would fall deeply into his muscular arms.

* * *

After dinner, Cathy kissed Harry good night and then returned to the kitchen to the kitchen to wash the dishes. Before she would finish, she knew that he would be dozing in his recliner, undisturbed. Her latest project was awaiting her in the garage, and she, too, wanted no distractions once she began working. Making fast work of the dishes, she dried her hands on a kitchen towel hanging from the oven door.

Collecting a soda from the refrigerator and her cigarette case, she entered the garage from the kitchen and was quite taken aback by what Harry had brought her. Time and the elements had taken their toll on what used to be a fashionable piece of furniture: a chest of drawers, probably made during the 1920s, Cathy surmised. The patina bore the scars of wear and neglect; the blackened, aged varnish covering all of the surfaces so that she could not readily discern what type of wood was used during its creation, but she imagined it to be oak.

One of the two top shallow drawers was missing a pull, and Cathy noticed a key hole whose key had probably landed into a junk box somewhere, the owner not knowing what it fit or where. The second drawer was pulled out and she could see that it had no bottom. She leaned over and pulled on the third drawer and the front fell off in her hands. When she tried to open the bottom drawer, she found that it was stuck. The short legs of the chest were on small casters, except for one, which caused the chest to tilt, cockeyed.

Cathy stepped back to survey this sagging eyesore and wondered if even she had enough vision to see it, as it should be. The whole chest reminded her of a face with one eye out and a jagged-toothed smile, leaning to one side. *Like a clown that's been punched out.*

She lit her cigarette as she pondered her next move. *Fix it or scrap it.* As she puffed lightly, she decided to try to repair the monstrosity and return a modicum of its dignity. A thin wisp of blue smoke curled upward as she placed her cigarette in the ashtray on her workbench. Taking a deep breath, she began removing the drawers and setting them to one side. Cathy chose a heavy screwdriver from her toolbox to use as a wedge to loosen the drawer that was stuck, but the stubborn wood was inflexible and refused to yield. I might just have to take it apart, she reasoned.

With a cleaning rag, she lovingly wiped all of the outside surfaces that she could. She thought of how almost a century ago, another woodcrafter had put love into his work for all to see: a pattern of grained woods. There, too, was no pressing need for him to spend those hours, but that pattern was his kiss of love for his craft. Cathy could see his hands passing over its smoothness, guided by the joy of the look and feel of it, and his hesitation to let it pass into the hands of a buyer.

She found stress relief in her efforts, allowing her to focus, which held anxiety or boredom at bay. Deeply, Cathy felt that wood, unlike iron, had a will of its own. Iron had to be heated and shaped, but working with wood required great attention, care, respect...and love. One incautious movement of the scraper could irreversibly scar a work, she believed, and the soul and spirit of the wood, itself, would find contempt in someone who feigned serious intent, and merely trifled with the work. Her strokes were cyclical and rhythmic, and each pass, confident.

The feel of the wood in her hands was soothing,

almost as if the wood, itself, were trying to speak to her, but she could only listen with her heart. Before she would realize it, her time-consuming efforts would reward her with visible progress. Cathy's concentration caused her to frequently lose track of time, and she would think, it's true...time does fly when you're having fun. Now that Michael and Heather were, more or less, self-sufficient, she found that she had quite a lot of time on her hands.

Positioning her body behind the wreckage, she gently lowered it to the concrete floor on its back. Cathy wiped her brow with the back of her hand and was surprised to find that she had broken a sweat. Her cigarette had extinguished itself, so she lit another as she sat down on the step at the door leading to the kitchen. A gulp of soda quenched her thirst as she silently inhaled and planned her next move.

She took a hammer and gently tapped the back of the drawer from the inside until the dovetail tenons separated. Following the same procedure at the front, she was able to remove the side of the drawer without splintering the wood. The strain from bending for so long caused her to stand up straight and rub the burning ache in her back. Heaving a sigh, she gave several massive pulls, and finally, the drawer slid out against its will. Straddling the chest, Cathy stuck her hand far back into the opening to see if she could determine what had lodged itself and had prevented the drawer from opening. Unable to ascertain, she jumped up and grabbed a flashlight from the workbench and knelt down on the cold concrete floor.

The obstacle located was a piece of wood nailed to the back of the chest. *Why would anyone nail a piece of wood here?* She bent over, peering at it with her flashlight. Her curiosity could not be contained. She knew that she must try to find out what long lost treasure from the twenties or thirties had been secured to the back of the chest behind the drawer. *Perhaps, it may be a treasure map,* and the prospect filled her with excitement. She tried to grasp it with her fingers, but found the object to be fixed in place, firmly, not meant to be removed. The value, not withstanding, was not the focus of her zeal. The thrill of discovery was the impetus that propelled her to fruition. She was not to be stymied.

She retrieved the screwdriver and deftly pushed up under the solid object. Prying upward caused nails to creak and she paused again and checked with her trusty flashlight.

Surely, this was not built like this. Her knees ached as she knelt on the floor with the flashlight. The yellow circle of light illuminated something that made her catch her breath. Secured behind three strips of wood was what appeared to be a small book, the top being the only part that was visible. *What is this?*

CHAPTER 3

"Cathy!" Harry called from the living room.

She raised up and dusted herself off, twisting slightly, trying to relieve the pain in her back. Her soda can was empty so she went to the kitchen for another.

"What?" she called upon entering.

"Are you ready to go to bed? The news is over and it's eleven-thirty."

"I'll wait for the kids to get in, then I'll be up."

"Heather's been home for thirty minutes, and she said that Michael went to the races and will be in around one," he called back.

Cathy had been so engrossed with the chest that the evening was gone and it was approaching midnight. Harry stretched as he got up and made his way to the stairs.

"I'm going back to bed," he said, "You coming?"

"I'll be in, in a minute," she answered, "I need to finish this up in the garage, and then I need to get in the shower."

He nodded affirmatively and made his way to the bedroom. She returned to the garage and lit another cigarette, studying the strips of wood that were nailed into blocks at the back of the frame. Somebody went to an awful lot of trouble to fix it this way, she mused, as she figured out a way to extract the book without damaging it or the chest. With hammer and screwdriver, she stealthily went at her work.

Thirty minutes had passed before she finally got the third strip of wood freed from the block and could finally see the object which rested on the back of the chest. She picked it up and as she tried to look at it, the garage light seemed dim compared to the flashlight. With book in hand, she got up and went into the kitchen where the fluorescent light was much brighter.

She gasped as she read the small letters at the bottom of the book's cover. *Diary.* The dusty black cover was loose and the small journal needed careful attention. *Oh, my gosh!* She painstakingly wiped the book with her kitchen towel, noting that it was quite fragile, indeed. She opened it to the middle, and at the top of the page read:

Thursday, July 28, 1938

Georgia Turner's baby died last night. The crib death. When she woke up it was gone. O, the sorrow in her home today. Poor Georgia is inconsolable.

Oh! My! Cathy was taken aback, as she gingerly closed the book and reopened it to the front where she found written in pale blue script, a name and a date: *Lynette Orenduff Stinson, 1938.*

Carefully, she turned the delicate page to January 1 and read

Saturday, January 1, 1938

Alma Connolly spent the day with me. This afternoon she and I went over to

see Mrs. Colbert. I enjoyed her visit very much. Tried to get her to stay until tomorrow.

Handwriting that had paled with time proved difficult to read, however, Georgia Turner's baby intrigued her. A nostalgic feeling began to overtake her, and even though she thought that she would find nothing earth-shattering in the little book, she ventured that it could make for some interesting reading. Quickly, she put her tools away, locked the doors, and turned off the lights before she made her way to her bedroom.

Harry had fallen asleep in bed while watching the television and was lightly snoring when Cathy showered and put on her pajamas. The diary lay on her nightstand and she thought that she would read it until she, too, fell asleep. Michael wasn't home yet, and she knew that she would be unable to sleep until he was.

Sitting up in bed, she positioned herself comfortably and opened the book that had not seen the light of day in decades. *Now, to January 2.*

Sunday, January 2, 1938

To S.S. and church. Brother Cash is very good. Nowhere this afternoon. To church tonight.

Oliver and Lee, Helen and William and Perry were here awhile tonight. We enjoy having them all come so much.

Cathy gave pause to consider these people: Oliver and Lee, Helen and William and Perry, and of course, Lynette, and thought it odd to see the names of real people who were probably all dead now. She rubbed her hand slowly across the diary's page and tried to formulate a mental image of Lynette, but so far, nothing came to mind.

S.S. Sunday School; pretty boring stuff. Yet she could not put the diary down for some reason. Curious about whom these people were and where they had lived, she speculated that if she kept on reading, she could garner clues from the brittle pages that would answer her questions. *I suppose that when Lynette wrote this, she never would have guessed that somebody would be reading it seventy years later.*

Monday, January 3, 1938

Went to Mrs. Graham's awhile this morning. She told me Baby was sick yesterday. So I went right on up there. Caught a way with Miss Fincher. Then came back with her. Got here about six o'clock. Ravanell stayed out of school today. Baby is better. I suppose she had a spell of tonsillitis. Mable had Dr. Warrenfells with Ravanell. He says it is her appendix.

Cathy strained her eyes reading the faded pages, trying to figure out Lynette's relationship to Mable, Ravanell, and Baby, and guessed the latter to be Lynette's children. *Lynette must be an older woman,* however, an innate feeling in her heart told her that this was not true. Her mind skipped and darted like a pinball bouncing off bumpers, making her feel intensely uncomfortable, as she kept trying to formulate a mental picture. Each time, the image would fade before she could grasp it, and the vagueness frustrated her.

Tuesday, January 4, 1938

This is a beautiful day. Ravanell is still suffering though. Dr. Warrenfells came about the middle of the day. Late this afternoon they took her to the hospital and operated on her. Mrs. Graham and I went up to see Mrs. Hammond, Mrs. Peacock, and Mrs. Shaw. Then we went to see Mrs. Cash. She was not home. Neither was Mrs. Peacock.

Wednesday, January 5, 1938

Mable stays at the hospital most of the time. Did a big washing today. Most of the things got dry. Mrs. Graham and I went to P.T.A. together. To prayer meeting tonight. I pray lots.

Thursday, January 6, 1938

It has rained nearly all day. Ned called to ask about Ravanell. He said Emily has been in bed all day. Ravanell is getting along all right. Had to borrow Mrs. Hosick's iron. Mine is down at K.C. Fox's for repairs.

Friday, January 7, 1938

Went down to Fox's this afternoon for my iron. Started over to see Emily, but stopped at the barber shop and asked Tommy about her. He said she is up to see Ravanell. Hattie Winslow stayed with Ravanell tonight and Mable stayed at home for the first time since Ravanell was operated on.

Puzzled, Cathy yawned and repositioned herself on her pillows. *If Ravanell is Lynette's daughter, why isn't she staying with her instead of Mable?* Having no notions or foreknowledge of the complicated cast of characters, she reached into her nightstand drawer for a tablet and pen to make a list with the intention of sorting it out later. She reminded herself that the petite volume was not a fiction book, and it could be that the story probably would have no plot and would make no sense to her at all. But, she concluded, there had to be some reason why Lynette had kept the diary, as well as hiding it so well. The quest had begun and she was now driven with dogged determination.

The sound of Michael's key in the front door lock momentarily interrupted her reading. She heard him bound up the stairs and his bedroom door close before she could tell him good night. However, rest would be easier, now that he was safe at home.

Her mind began to wander again, this time to thoughts of her children. Until this time in her life, Cathy had given little thought to herself or her concerns. When she had been a new wife, Harry had been the primary focus in her life. When she became a mother, her children had commanded all of her time, as well as her thoughts. Now, however, all of this was changed, and the strange and new status quo alarmed and confused her. Her cause and effect relationship with her children, the product of years of trial and error, constituted a relationship that was straightforward, and at the same time, complicated. Sometimes, she felt as though the empty nest syndrome, which made up her inert existence, was exceptionally cruel, but no one could understand it unless they'd been through it.

She spent a good deal of her time in imaginary kingdoms. Castles in the clouds and fairy tale pursuits had replaced baby books, talk shows, and self-help gurus. The tough and demanding questions that had plagued her, and related far too closely to the discomfort of her daily life, could not break the illusion of this celestial world that she had created; a world where her problems always found perfect solutions. Shaking her head and settling back to task, the old diary reclaimed her attention.

Saturday, January 8, 1938

Nothing special today. No chance to read and study though. Went to Miss Mary Lizzie's about six o'clock. Mable is in and out everyday.

Sunday, January 9, 1938

To S.S. and church today. Did not get to go up home this afternoon though I wanted to very much. Mr. Allen Pettigrew is a corpse at Hosick's. I went over there this afternoon. Went to church tonight. Dr. Pierce preached and held the Quarterly meeting.

Cathy was elated. *At last! A clue! Hosick's is a funeral home. Now, if I can find out where.* She felt a small vibration in her fingertips, as though she were on to something. She wrote the name Hosick Funeral Home on a clean page of the tablet and drew a line under it. Under the line, she wrote Allen Pettigrew, having no idea how many names would be listed by the time she reached the page about Georgia Turner's baby.

Glancing up at the blank screen of her computer monitor, she knew that the lateness of the hour would preclude her from beginning her search. However, her heart was in it now, and she knew that sooner or later she'd figure it all out. Riddles and puzzles had always interested her, and she wiled away many an hour solving them. This would be no different. She just needed to take the time to gather as many clues as she could, until all of the puzzle pieces would fit and she could view the entire picture.

The air of mystery, the unknown, was alluring, and she often wondered if there were any others who felt as she did. Harry always said that she was unique, and had missed her calling in life. In his opinion, Cathy should have been a detective. Though her eyelids were growing heavy, she yawned and stretched, and decided to read a few more pages.

Monday, January 10, 1938

Wanted to go up home so very much today, but I did not get off. Ravanell is still in the hospital. Think she will come back tomorrow probably. Mrs. Massey and Betty June came over awhile tonight.

Tuesday, January 11, 1938

Mable called this morning and asked me to build a fire. Said they would bring Ravanell. She came about 10 o'clock. I had early dinner and went up home on the 12 o'clock bus. Baby brought me back.

Emily came by tonight as she was going to the hospital. She is to be operated on tomorrow.

Wednesday, January 12, 1938

When I got through with dinner today I went up to see how Emily is getting along. She is still sick from the ether. Mable went to the show. Ned came to see Ravanell. I went to Prayer Meeting. Charles went too.

Cathy directed her glance toward the clock and mentally calculated how many hours she could sleep, which she already knew would not be enough, before she arose at six. Her gaze fell on Harry, and her expression was no less than adoration, but she did not wake him.

She was still held captive to the past and the diary would not let her go just yet. Her mind played tricks on her, and she kept reminding herself that this was not a story, that these were real people, and she should not expect too much to come forth. Still, the voices from the past seemed to beckon her. The element of expectancy that she had felt all day seemed to be assuaged with the discovery of the diary. She felt now that it had been meant for her to find it, as everything happens for a reason. *There are no accidents. Each incident has a purpose in life, each thread in the tapestry. But, what is the purpose?*

Perhaps, she would find the answers to some of her urgent and crucial expressions of inquiry, or perhaps, there were life lessons she needed to learn. Or, perhaps, she would be the instrument through which another could find solace. She knew of no sure way of determining the outcome, but was intrigued with 1938, and felt fortunate to have found a firsthand account.

Thursday, January 13, 1938

Went to see Emily this afternoon and to see Miss Mary Lizzie. She is not so well.

Friday, January 14, 1938

The Children of the Confederacy met with Charles this afternoon. I enjoyed fixing for it. Mable helped me to serve.

Cathy read and reread this entry, and then wrote it down on the pad. The Children of the Confederacy meant that Lynette was from the South. *But, where? Probably, Georgia ... yes, perhaps south Georgia.* Her eye caught the clock on her bedside table again and this time, she relented, as she had to work tomorrow.

Harry was still snoring as Cathy pulled a slip of paper from the nightstand drawer and marked her place in the diary. She'd take it with her tomorrow and read it on her lunch break, she decided. Lynette, Mable, Ravanell, Baby, and all of the others stirred around in her thoughts as she fell asleep. Perhaps, she had been wrong about Lynette's age. Maybe, Lynette was a much older woman with grown children. Old or not, it seemed to Cathy that Lynette had been a God-fearing, churchgoing woman, yet not so maternal with her own children, if they were hers.

These might not even be her children, Cathy thought as she drifted off to sleep.

Maybe Lynette was the housekeeper.

* * *

Shadowy figures sat in front of a fireplace. The Children of the Confederacy. To Sunday School and church...a schoolboy listening to the radio...Mrs. Hammond, Mrs. Peacock, and Mrs. Shaw...Miss Mary Lizzie...and Mable, Ravanell...and Lynette. Who are you, Lynette?

CHAPTER 4

Music from her radio alarm blared at what seemed to be earlier than usual, but as Cathy turned it off, she noted that it was, indeed, six o'clock. She felt inert and sluggish, but got up anyway and went to the kitchen to make breakfast before leaving for work. She readied herself quietly so as not to wake Harry or the kids. Dressed in scrubs, she hurriedly ate her oatmeal and drank coffee. The Chattanooga autumn mornings were chilly now, so she filled her auto cup with the steaming liquid and zipped up her jacket, not forgetting to slip the diary into her purse before she walked out the door.

Traffic was heavy at the ridge cut, but slowly and methodically she made her way to Germantown Road and through the tunnel to McCallie Avenue. The silhouette of the tall red brick structure of Erlanger Hospital loomed in the distance and Cathy knew that when she saw Erlanger, she was not far from the nursing home. Maybe I'll have some time, she thought, to read a little bit more of the diary.

Day was not yet breaking when Cathy parked her car. Without thinking, she punched the building code on the keypad and entered the silent building to clock in for her shift. She rode the elevator and walked out onto the second floor with her coworker of the past eight years, Georgina Pack, Gigi, for short. The pair chatted casually as they made their way to their workstation.

Ten years' Cathy's junior, Gigi walked purposefully, paying little attention to their surroundings, her long black hair cascading in well-calculated ringlets down her back. Of Latin descent, her well-tanned coloring complemented her light blue scrubs and serviceable white shoes. Appearing to be the same height, Cathy found that she envied Gigi's petite size and her ability to eat practically anything she wanted without ever gaining an ounce. Cathy, on the other hand, had struggled for more than a year to lose twenty pounds.

Eight years ago, Gigi had moved to Chattanooga from Miami, and had begun immediately to search for employment, which proved to be disappointing. Her fortuitous encounter with Cathy occurred during a sudden rainstorm when she had dashed into The Second Cup seeking shelter. Not realizing that anyone was on the other side of the door, she had pushed headlong, almost knocking Cathy down, and sending Cathy's coffee splattering onto the floor.

Graciously, Cathy had accepted her profuse apologies as she wiped her clothes and hands with napkins retrieved from a nearby table. Gigi had offered to buy her another cup, and when Cathy had accepted, a horrified look had come over the drenched girl's face and her lips had begun to tremble.

Taking her gently by the arm, Cathy steered her toward the nearby table, and as the two sat, Gigi had begun to cry. Two cups of coffee later, Cathy had heard Gigi's story of her inability to find a job and no money with which to replace the spilled coffee. When she learned that they shared the same interests and occupational skills, she mentioned Shepherd-of-the-Hills, and that she would put in a recommendation for her. Two weeks later, the two were teamed on the second floor where they had worked since; Cathy, empathic and compassionate, and Gigi, quick-witted and capable.

Gigi pulled a piece of paper from her pocket and began crossing off names as they started their shift. Breakfast was being delivered and the time had come to awaken the residents for the day. Cathy hoped that she would not have to waken Mrs. Pickelsimer, a most disagreeable woman.

"You feed Mr. Mack, Mrs. Leach, Mrs. Strain, and Mrs. Peacock, and I'll take Mrs. Pickelsimer, Mrs. Graham, Mr. Barnes, and Mr. Cain...okay? Gigi glanced sidewise as she spoke.

"Sounds good to me," Cathy answered, "Mrs. Pickelsimer can't stand me anyway."

Gigi quipped, "I don't think Mrs. Pickelsimer can get along with anybody," as she removed a tray from the breakfast cart. Cathy nodded in agreement, taking a tray and quietly entering Mr. Mack's room. She set the tray on his bed table.

"Mr. Mack," she said, softly, gently shaking his shoulder. The old man stirred and Cathy handed him his glasses.

"Who're you?" his graveled voice asked.

Cathy identified herself to him twice, as Jarvis entered the room. She knew that because of Mr. Mack's age and mental degeneration, this was going to be "one of those days." She excused herself so Jarvis could help Mr. Mack with his morning toileting, and returned after taking meal trays to Mrs. Leach, Mrs. Strain, and Mrs. Peacock.

She waited patiently outside Mr. Mack's door until Jarvis signaled her that they had finished.

He carefully lowered Mr. Mack into his recliner and set the tray table in front of him. Cathy set his breakfast tray before him before she positioned herself comfortably in a chair beside him. As she prepared to feed him, she noticed that the elderly gentleman was awake, yet not fully alert.

"I'll be back soon, Mr. Mack," Jarvis reassured him, "Cathy will take good care of you until I get back." Mr. Mack did not allow himself to feel any curiosity about Jarvis's direction. Cathy smiled at Mr. Mack, but he just looked at her pensively. Jarvis thanked her and backed out the door.

Lifting the top from his entree, she said, "It's bacon and eggs, and toast and jelly. Yummy, you'll like that!"

"We'll see about that," his voice crackled.

"I make pretty good bacon, myself," Cathy tried to make conversation. Mr. Mack was not moved, so Cathy silently fed him, and as he ate, he eyed her suspiciously.

"White trash," he muttered.

"Mr. Mack," Cathy addressed the old man softly, "You've only been here two days and I don't know of you being nice to anyone. Is there anything wrong? I know you don't want to be here, but we're not here to hurt you...we only want to help you."

So says you!" he retorted.

As he slowly chewed, a bit of egg dribbled down his chin, and Cathy tenderly wiped it for him. She then picked up his juice and held the straw so that he could drink easily.

"Your bacon's prob'ly better'n this soy crap," he criticized.

"Well, mine is pretty good," Cathy smiled, "I think the secret is to cook it slowly. I always try to make good breakfasts."

"The best'uns I ever et was back in the twenties," he began, "My mama was the best cook in the county."

"She sounds wonderful," Cathy said, pleasantly, "Tell me about her."

"Not much to tell," he paused, and Cathy could tell from his gaze that, momentarily, he was back in his youth. "We lived on the ole Brickyard Road, just outside LaFayette, over in Walker County. Mama died in '27. One day, she just up an' keeled over."

"I'm sorry," Cathy consoled, "How old were you?"

"No more'n a teenager, myself...thirteen. Daddy died when I was fo' an' Mama depended on me fo' ever'thin'."

"What did you do after she passed away?" Cathy's curiosity was piqued.

"I's workin' at the gin fo' Mr. Marcus then, so's I jest kept workin' there."

"Was it a cotton gin?" Cathy asked, softly.

"Yes," he stared across the room, "Trammel's gin...an' the grist mill. He owned th' house, but as I's workin' fo' him, he let us stay there...me, an' Thad, an' my sister."

"Just the three of you?"

Mr. Mack nodded his head. Jarvis had heard Mr. Mack and Cathy talking, so he quietly entered the room and took a seat in the corner. Cathy dipped some oatmeal and slowly lifted the spoon to Mr. Mack's lips. He did not resist her efforts and turned his head toward her. Her warm smile seemed to put him at ease.

"Was Mr. Trammel good to you, Mr. Mack?" she asked.

"Mr. Marcus good 'nuf," his voice was muffled as Cathy wiped his mouth, "But, back then, a colored person couldn't really trust no white man. Not fo' a fair shake, anyways."

"What do you mean?"

"Well," his voice trailed, momentarily, "Like I says, I's workin' there fo' Mr. Marcus, an' done anythin' and ever'thin' Mr. Marcus say do. Mr. Clyde, from up to th' dairy, used to come down to the mill to see Mr. Marcus. E've'body knowed that Mr. Marcus and Mr. Clyde made moon...out back o' th' mill. My first cousin, Thad, and me worked the still, but we didn't make no deliveries."

Cathy and Jarvis were mesmerized by the old man's tale. "Go on," Cathy prodded him.

"Mr. Clyde would send th' milk truck down to pick up th' moon and it would be delivered with th' milk," Mr. Mack laughed at the memory. "Worked purty good fo' awhile, but soon 'nuf them agents catch on and come to bust up th' still."

"Were Mr. Marcus and Mr. Clyde arrested?" Jarvis inquired.

"Sho 'nuf," he snorted, "An' th' same fo' me an' Thad. Well, we come up fo' this judge in LaFayette. Mean bastard. Give me an' Thad a year in the county lockup for makin' moon. Had to work that chain gang out toward Pea Vine, no matter what th' weather."

"What happened to Mr. Marcus and Mr. Clyde?" Jarvis piped.

"Nuthin' happ'n," Mr. Mack spat out the words bitterly, "Story wuz that Judge's daughter wuz sweet on Mr. Marcus, so Judge fined 'im a hunnert dollars. But, Mr. Clyde...it cost him right more. Seems like, if I rec'lect, right after me and Thad went to jail, Judge married Mr. Clyde's daughter. A pretty, young girl. I felt right bad fo' her. Guess he bought her."

"That wasn't right," Cathy murmured.

Sitting forward in his chair, he turned to Cathy and Jarvis, "But, I haven't trusted no white man since!"

"You can trust me," Cathy reassured him.

"Not fo' my bath," Mr. Mack retorted, and Cathy knew that it was time for her to go. She rose and Jarvis smiled and shook his head. Cathy closed the door softly behind her, leaving Jarvis to attend to Mr. Mack and his bath.

Breakfasting, washing, toileting, cleaning, and bathing all conspired against Cathy and her quest to read the diary. Her whole morning, as well as lunch, seemed to be at least half an hour off her regular schedule. It was late afternoon before Gigi covered her for her break so she could go out to the patio to smoke a cigarette. She slipped the diary and her cigarette case into her pocket, checked all of her patients, and then quickly made her way to the smoking area.

Finding a corner table, she welcomed the time to get off her feet, and lit a cigarette as she sat down. Exhaling, she quickly found her place and began to read, despite overcast skies and gathering autumn shadows.

Saturday, January 15, 1938

Baby came as usual. Went down to see Mrs. Cash awhile this afternoon. Also to see Emily.

Delicately handling the yellowed pages, she kept losing her place whenever curious co-workers came by, trying to peer at what she was reading. She was not yet ready to share this find with anyone until she knew more about it.

Sunday, January 16, 1938

To S.S. and church. To see Miss Mary Lizzie a couple of times. This afternoon to see Emily, then to see Gladys. She had her tonsils taken out Friday. Then over to see Mrs. Hanson who has been sick for quite a while. Charles and I went to church tonight. Oliver and Lee came awhile tonight.

Monday, January 17, 1938

To see Emily this morning and to see Miss Mary Lizzie this afternoon. Miss Jessie and Miss Dixie came to see Ravanell tonight.

Charles is so sweet to me. I love him so very much.

The last sentence surprised and perplexed her. *Charles? Who is Charles? Now, this is getting interesting. Husband? Child?* Cathy pulled out a small notebook she used to record patients' vitals and once again wrote the names of Lynette's friends, family, and associates, as she had written on the tablet on her nightstand. As she identified them, she had decided to write what she knew about each one beside their name, and try to determine if a pattern existed.

Let's see, Lynette, Mable, Ravanell, Baby, Charles, she wrote, and listed the names she had encountered thus far. She mentally calculated that if Ravanell had had appendicitis in 1938, it was entirely possible that she could still be alive somewhere. If Charles were a child, he, too, could be alive and well somewhere, as well.

Mesmerized in these moments, her break was over all too quickly, so she prepared to go inside.

Cathy felt a sprinkling of rain and hurriedly shut the little book, almost with a look of pain on her face. She darted under the awning and tucked the diary carefully into her pocket while she stood for a moment and finished her cigarette. A gust of bitter wind seemed to cut through her clothing, chilling her to the bone, and her eyes pensively searched the disquieting clouds that had joined forces with the wind.

She heaved a sigh as she entered the building, her shift twelve hours, as the facility was short-staffed. She liked to walk down the quiet halls and admire the artwork, as well as the decor, and felt soothed by the quiet atmosphere and cleanliness that always prevailed at the facility. The tranquil order of Shepherd-of-the-Hills stood bravely against the chaos and adversity, so much that peace and tranquility would eventually give way to boredom.

As she passed the activities room, she peered through the broad windows to see Mr. Peacock fumbling with her walker as she stumbled among the chairs and tables. The room was shadowy, even though the crisp October nights had thinned the vines above the windows, and some of the broad five-fingered leaves of the creepers were stained crimson, clinging with tiny appendages to the brick on the outside of the building. An aide soon appeared and hurriedly guided the old woman to wherever she was supposed to be; not that Mrs. Peacock had known where she was, in the first place.

Cathy's gaze was drawn beyond Mrs. Peacock to Mrs. Leach, who was seated at a metal table drawn close to the opposite window, struggling, it appeared, to make wax flowers. She seemed to be deeply depressed, and her frustration at being unable to properly manipulate her clumsy, trembling hands showed on her tired face. Even she could see that the red spirals that she had stuck to the shaky green stems were as unlike the flowers she had meant to make, as the painted smell of the softened wax was unlike the lilting fragrance of spring roses.

Knowing that she could not offer the woman aid nor comfort, Cathy walked slowly back to her workstation where Jarvis stopped her in the hallway. "Hey, Cathy, thanks for helping me with Mr. Mack this morning. I was pretty backed up, and I needed the help."

Cathy admired his smile of genuine appreciation and nodded.

"Hey," he added before departing, "Don't let those comments Mr. Mack made this morning get next to you. He's just generational...you know?"

"Don't worry about it, Jarvis," she smiled, "I've been called worse. Besides, Harry's home and it would take a lot more than that to spoil my weekend."

They laughed and parted company, and Cathy hurried to resume her work. She was looking forward to sleeping late, and she was looking forward to Harry.

As she walked across the parking lot at the end of her shift, Gigi called out to her and threw up her hand to wave. Evening was passing and a cold night lay ahead, heralded by a stiff wind. Cathy pulled her jacket collar tighter around her neck, and she wished that she had worn a heavier coat. The elements would tax her until she was safe at home where she could be warm and cozy...and she could cuddle with Harry.

CHAPTER 5

Cathy looked forward to this weekend and this October, but Harry did not share her curiosity and zeal for living. She did not want life to become ordinary, and was open to any reveries that Harry might suggest. Since he spent so much time on the road, he really didn't like to go out, and Cathy planned her time around the house when he was home.

This weekend, she spent her time laundering and house cleaning. The ensuing week, amid pumpkins, skeletons, and spider webs, brought quiet evenings with Harry, as well as intermittent interactions with her children.

Heather and Angela consumed their time decorating the front of the house and the front yard for Halloween. Cathy had always enjoyed the holiday when her children were young, but it did not mean so much to her nowadays. Her hope was to, one day, cook a meal that everybody liked, and they could all sit down together as a family, the way they used to do. However, Michael and Heather were not amicable to the notion, and Cathy had no idea how she could get their lives to mesh.

Harry reassured her that this distance was just part of their growing up processes, so Cathy busied herself cooking for Harry: corned beef and cabbage, beef stew, fried chicken, and a host of delectable side dishes to accompany the entrees. Her kitchen was warm and comfortable, and she and Harry felt close as they dined alone at the kitchen table.

Sometimes after dinner, she and Harry would take a walk around the block, enjoying the autumn evenings when the temperature was permissible. Most of the time, however, Harry liked to relax in his recliner and Cathy would retreat to her workshop in the garage.

Thursday evening while she worked on the antique chest, a sudden tiredness overtook her, so much that it caused her to lean against the chest and hold on so as not to fall. She quickly backed up and sat down on the steps for this feeling was concurrently familiar and unfamiliar, and she feared that she might lose all consciousness. That was not the case as the entrancing illusion captivated her. She did not want to look, but she found that she could not turn away.

The face before her was blurred, and she could not readily make out the features. As the image became clearer, Cathy could tell that the woman was not old, but looked weary. Her eyes were sunken into their sockets and the gaunt expression on her face foretold her lack of sleep. She seemed to be a pitiable creature, and Cathy sensed melancholy about her.

The vision widened and Cathy strained to see what appeared to be gray blotches around the woman. As the objects came into focus, she realized that they were headstones, and that the melancholy woman was standing in a cemetery. The surroundings were unfamiliar to Cathy and she was unable to make out any of the names on the stones. Somehow, this weary, sorrowful woman and this ancient place had transcended Time, and had reached out from the past to contact her.

In an instant, the images began to fade, and Cathy tried to hold them in her mind as long as possible. Alone in the garage, she was stunned at what she had just *seen*, and the fragments flitted silently, until the entire vision was beyond her grasp. She shook her head quickly, looking around. Slowly, she rose and stood up and walked slowly back to the chest. A tingling sensation went through her fingers when she touched it, and a wave of excitement washed over her. *This woman was somehow connected to this chest!* The thought at having received an image from another era through time and space overwhelmed her and gave her a great surge of energy.

"Harry! Harry!" she cried as she burst through the door. She stopped short at the living room, as she found that Harry had, once again, fallen asleep in his recliner. Frustrated, she wanted to wake him so that he could share this moment, but somehow felt it lacked an interest for him, if he even believed her. So, she opted to let him sleep. He slept without worry, snoring softly.

Surprised at how much time had elapsed, she found the evening was gone and decided to stop her work for the night. Her plan now was to take a nice warm shower, don fresh night clothes, and settle back and read the diary.

When she came out of the bathroom, she noticed that Harry had come to bed and had already fallen asleep watching television. She thought it just as well, for she wanted to get back to reading the diary, so she dressed for bed quickly. Harry had already locked the doors and turned out the lights, so Cathy walked softly down the hall, peeked in to say good night to Michael and Heather, and made her way back to her bedroom.

Sitting up in bed on fluffed-up pillows, book in hand, she stopped for a moment to listen to the low moan of the wind through sparsely-leafed trees. The eerie sound sent shivers up her spine, and she felt a contentedness that her family was settled for the night. A silent prayer of thankfulness to God suddenly went through her mind, and a peacefulness overtook her. She found her place and began to read.

Tuesday, January 18, 1938

Mable went to Chattanooga this afternoon. Ravanell is up now. She walked to the kitchen this afternoon. Emily was carried home today.

Wednesday, January 19, 1938

Went to the Presbyterian church tonight to hear a missionary from China. Ravanell goes to the table for her meals now.

Thursday, January 20, 1938

Went to see Emily this afternoon. She is getting along all right.

Friday, January 21, 1938

Lucile received a message today that Ross had been operated on in Greenville, S.C. for appendicitis. The appendix is ruptured. She went immediately. Her father and mother I suppose will go with her. Miss Mary Lizzie and I have a session of prayer together as often as I can go over.

Saturday, January 22, 1938

Lucile called Helen this morning. Ross is doing as well as could be expected. [C!] went with her. She said they would stay a few days to see how he gets along.

As Cathy wrote down the new names she had read, mental images began to form and she was under the impression that Ross must be Lucile's brother. She felt a surge of excitement that Lynette's home seemed to be in the proximity of Chattanooga, but there were numerous small towns and communities in the area, and she could not imagine which one it might be. *It could even be a town so old that it no longer exists! A diary from here, and it makes it all the way back from Cedartown, Georgia. Coincidence?*

Sunday, January 23, 1938

To S.S. and church today. Nowhere this afternoon. Wanted to go up home very much but couldn't get off. James and Willard came home with Charles from church today. They stayed until about five o'clock. Tonight Jimmy, Kerry, and Seab and Charles sat in Mable's room and played a game. Ravanell and Ned sat in the parlor. Helen, William, Oliver, Lee, and Sadie and Gladys sat in our room and visited Judge. Charles and I went to church tonight. Brother Keith preached his last sermon today.

Cathy reflected for a few moments. *Sunday School and church, Sunday School and church...that's all they ever do.* With each new bit of boring information, she was now under the impression that Lynette could have been a domestic, what with her references to not being able to get off to go "up home," wherever "up home" was, and Judge must be her employer. Since Ned had once again come to see Ravanell, she deduced that he must be her boyfriend. Before long, nagged by a slight hunger and restlessness, Cathy went to the kitchen for a soda and snack.

Lynette must be the housekeeper or something. She nibbled on popcorn as she read. The list on the page in the little notebook was getting longer, but few relationships were recorded next to the names. Cathy sipped her soda and lit another cigarette before turning the page. Her thoughts were droll and she tried to develop a course of their conversation in her head, but to no avail. *Maybe, this is just a boring account of someone's boring life.*

Monday, January 24, 1938

To the circle meeting this afternoon at Mrs. Bledsoe's.

Tuesday, January 25, 1938

I wanted to get the twelve o'clock bus to go up home today, but could not get dinner ready so I just got a taxi about one o'clock. Baby brought me back.

Tonight Mable would not let Charles listen to Orphan Annie. Nothing special she wanted but she was just determined he shouldn't listen to what he wanted. She has it all day long and as late as she wants it at night, but she won't give in for him to get what he wants for just fifteen minutes.

Wednesday, January 26, 1938

Thermometer around 20° this morning. Cold all day. Water frozen. Carried water from Mrs. Hosick's. Charles and I went to Prayer meeting tonight.

Charles bought a hot plate for my birthday present. Bless his sweet soul. Nothing from Judge. One would reason that a birthday would justify an acknowledgment, but Judge's absorption in self does not allow him to care for anyone around him.

Charles gave me an electric hot plate for a birthday present. Charles went over to Miss Mary Lizzie's to listen to Little Orphan Annie.

A curious smile of recognition played on Cathy's lips as she wrote furiously. She knew "Little Orphan Annie" to be a radio program from the thirties. Charles must be a little boy, she thought but still had no clue as to his relationship to Mable, Ravanell, and Lynette. Having accepted the quest of the diary, Cathy knew that she would have to see it through to the end, no matter how bland it might become. Even though she could not control the outcome, at least she could dominate the process. An innate force that she knew had been with her since her childhood would drive her to completion, no matter what the task.

Thursday, January 27, 1938

Still very cold. Have not washed this week. Do not know whether I can wash tomorrow. Charles has gone to a candy pulling at the church tonight. Charles and I bring all the water we use from Mrs. Hosick. He got up all of his lessons this afternoon. O, God! May my faith in Thee not waver as I pass through the testing time of life. [See opposite page]

Her interest lacking aggression, Cathy peered at the opposite page. Brackets contained the notes about the birthday present that Charles had bought for Lynette, as well as the passage about going to Miss Mary Lizzie's to listen to Little Orphan Annie on the radio. She was sure now that Charles was a schoolboy.

* * *

In the middle of the night, she awoke. Her bedroom seemed to be twice its size and Cathy felt disoriented. A glow flickered from the coal oil lamp on the mantelpiece. An old woman was reclining in a large bed, and a woman was sleeping in an armchair beside it. Cathy did not recognize her and leaned over the edge of her bed to have a better view of her features that were illuminated by the flickering light of the lamp.

It seemed to her, though, that she had seen her face before. But, when? But, where? The woman was slumbering peacefully with her head slumped on her shoulder and her Bible open on her lap. She was not heavily built, but of sufficient stature that she was not sickly or weak. Her large hands fell on either side of the chair. Bewildered, Cathy looked at the woman steadily.

Of course! She had seen her face! Had it been recently? She could not remember, and the puzzle excited and troubled her. She crept out of bed noiselessly to take a look at the sleeper, and approached her on tiptoe. She was the woman she had seen in the cemetery! Now, she was confused. Had she met her before, at another time in her life? Or, was it she only imagined she recognized her; and how had she come into her room...and why?

* * *

The alarm clock startled her to complete consciousness, and she sat bolt upright in bed. Disarming the device of its harsh noise, she sat shaking. Looking around her room, she had to make sure that it had been just a dream, *yes, a dream,* she told herself. Cathy was surprised to find that she had been perspiring profusely, and her hair was soaked.

Friday, Friday, she repeated in her mind, trying to orient herself to her surroundings. The dream grew more and more distant before she could write it down, and it had completely disappeared by the time she showered.

CHAPTER 6

Shortly past noon, Cathy and Gigi walked down the hallway to the cafeteria for their lunch trays. The diary will have to wait again, Cathy thought, as she and Gigi found a table close to the television so they could watch while they ate.

"You seemed to be pretty preoccupied this week, Cat," Gigi began, "Anything wrong?"

"No, no, I've just been busy...that's all," she answered the quiz, not wanting to explain her frustration at being too busy with her family and with Harry being home, and not finding sufficient time to read the diary.

Cathy's cell phone rang, and she hurriedly fished around in her pocket until she found it. It was Harry and she was dismayed to learn that he had been dispatched to make an emergency run to California and would be gone for four days. She understood, yet understanding did little to alleviate her disappointment, which she made a concerted effort to mask. She kissed Harry good-bye over the phone with his promise to call her before he went to sleep, as she was not looking forward to another Friday night alone.

"Is everybody all right?"

"Oh, sure, everybody's fine. Harry's got to go to California. You know how it goes when you don't get a day off and you can't seem to find enough time to get everything done and when you do, you're too tired to do it," Cathy laughed.

Gigi nodded in agreement, "I know what you mean. I don't even have kids, just Fred, and I still don't have time to do everything."

As they dined, Cathy noticed Gigi staring across the room. Shepherd-of-the-Hills employees had begun milling about, seeking tables upon which to set their trays. Cathy looked up to the large screen of the television, peripherally eyeing the pensive look on Gigi's face.

"What is it, Gigi?" Cathy inquired, taking a bite of casserole.

"Look...through that crowd."

Cathy peered around a group of multicolored scrubs, unable to see what was causing Gigi's distress. She did see an old woman whom she knew, and wished she didn't. It was Mrs. Pickelsimer, aged and bent over her walker, shuffling toward the doorway.

"What's Mrs. Pickelsimer doing down here?" she puzzled.

"That's what I'd like to know," Gigi snapped, "She's not supposed to be off the floor. I wonder how she got out. I don't see anybody with her."

The clicking of her walker ceased and became muffled thuds as she slowly and surely advanced through the open doorway. Her flannel gown held sway with the rhythm of the walker, and her scuffed, pink vinyl house shoes whispered as they slid across the carpet.

Cathy and Gigi could read no spark of recognition in her eyes, and as she neared the table, Gigi tried to capture her attention. But, her efforts were in vain.

Mrs. Pickelsimer did not seem to hear her. She maintained her faraway gaze, unobservant of the goings-on around her, and then took a stiff step backward. Her hand came up from her walker, as though to shield her eyes, and then, suddenly, she seemed to spin around. She fell, escaping the corner of a table as if by a miracle, to the floor of the dining hall. Her neck stiffened in horrified cognizance, stifling an involuntary cry.

Gigi was the first one up. Cathy and several others soon joined her to attend to Mrs. Pickelsimer. In an effort to assist in her part of this endeavor, Cathy dropped to her knees and took the old woman's hand, searching for a pulse, while Gigi checked for any sign of breath.

Through all of the commotion, Cathy heard a voice on the intercom, and soon the dining area was flooded with medical personnel, as well as administration. A "Do Not Resuscitate" order was on file, as per Mrs. Pickelsimer's wishes, so no lifesaving measures were taken, and the medical attendants quickly removed the frail body from the floor to the emergency ward.

Expected or not, it was an unpleasant fact: Mrs. Pickelsimer was dead. Adrenaline and surprise had left a bitter taste in Cathy's mouth, and she found, as she and Gigi sat back down, that she no longer had any appetite.

This was the way it usually was when one of the seniors passed. Cathy found that at these moments, there was no shock, only surprise. Just as in this moment with Mrs. Pickelsimer, the event, in itself, was surprising because Cathy didn't feel any emotion, except that which was urgent to activity; to do something that must be done to prolong a life. At the moment of the elder's demise, however, there was nothing that anyone could do; the silver thread connecting soul to body had broken, and her departure was swift.

The investigation into Mrs. Pickelsimer's death had begun, and all it did was to add to everyone's responsibilities. The culmination, however, would be as always: again, someone would be singled out and held accountable for negligence, and then somebody's employment would be terminated, at the very least. Security would be heightened and procedures would be scrutinized. The unfortunate overworked individual who had been in charge of Mrs. Pickelsimer at the time she walked off would be the fodder of the second-floor gossip mill for a while, before sinking into oblivion...or prosecution.

Whenever one of the residents would expire, the specter of the episode would usually stay with Cathy for a day or so. She would spend her moments reflecting and projecting: thinking about what had been given and what had been taken for granted, lest she should fall in with the guilty. During the empty subsequent days, she would enrich her life by changing her perspective of her everyday surroundings; the way she looked at things—a colored leaf, a group of white birches, a dilapidated barn, a golden iris, a robin hopping about on the lawn, or the taste of slices of tender, succulent chicken.

Despite the hectic morning and their chaotic lunchtime, the charge nurse sent an aide for Gigi and Cathy to come to help turn a patient after lunch. Cathy hoped that the worst part of her day was behind her, and now only looked forward to the end of her shift. She was tired, her energy spent. All she wanted to do now was to get home and recharge her physical and emotional batteries. Little did she know that her day would be further taxed by the episode with Miss Epperson, the largest woman that Cathy had ever seen.

* * *

Miss Epperson lay on her bed, and Cathy had never seen a human being so huge in all of her life. She appeared to be two eyes, a nose, and a mouth, floating and sinking, and floating again, on a pallid sea of fat that spread out, covering most of her bed.

From her chart, Cathy learned that the obese patient was only in her twenties, and suffered from an extensive list of weight-related illnesses. The scene stirred her heart, but Gigi was not so comforting or compassionate. She and Gigi quietly stepped out of the room to discuss the situation at hand.

"Her chart says her last weight was recorded as five hundred and twenty-two pounds," Cathy whispered in Gigi's ear.

Gigi's eyes cut a sidewise glance. "Five hundred, my foot," she whispered back, "She's probably pushing six...if not more."

"She probably can't help herself."

But, Gigi was not to be moved. "She should have helped herself when she only weighed three hundred pounds and could still walk. Nobody told her to keep eating herself to death."

"Maybe, it's genetic," Cathy suggested, "A lot of people are predisposed to be obese. You know that."

"Hey, you know what they say: Your genetics might load the gun, but your fork pulls the trigger," Gigi rolled her eyes, emphatically, "She should've backed off the pork chops a long time ago."

Cathy pursed her lips and shook her head, smiling, "Well, what're we going to do?"

Gigi looked at her, shaking her head, "We need more help."

At that moment, she spied Jarvis coming down the hall. He greeted them with a wide smile as he approached Miss Epperson's room. A pleasing character, he was tall and wiry, yet under his chocolate skin, untold muscles would not allow him to be put off by unpleasant tasks. His very presence seemed to put everyone at ease and he seemed to know exactly what to do and when to do it. Not given to a caustic nature, the residents felt secure when Jarvis was there, and his passion for his patients was heartfelt; his concern, genuine.

"Good afternoon, ladies," he proffered, "What have we got going on down here today? Hazel said you needed some help."

"Clarissa and Elaine need to turn Miss Epperson and change her bedding," Cathy began, "And, really, Jarvis, I don't know how we're going to do it. I don't think we've ever had anyone as heavy as this before."

Jarvis craned his neck and peered into the room. He drew back and by his pained expression, Cathy could tell that he had never handled a patient of these proportions before, either. A furrow formed in his brow as he formulated his next question.

"Can she stand up?" he queried.

"No," Cathy answered immediately, "According to her chart, her abdominal panniculus is Grade Five, and even if she could stand up, the panniculus would hang to her knees. She wouldn't be able to straighten up enough to distribute her weight, and her legs wouldn't be able to support her. They'd probably break."

Gigi rolled her eyes, "There are five of us here, and frankly, I don't think we'll be able to do it."

"Let me go get a lift," Jarvis offered.

"I don't think we have a lift that will sustain that much weight," Cathy said.

"Well, if it won't lift her, maybe we can use it to help turn her," he answered as he walked back up the hallway.

Clarissa and Elaine joined them in the hallway and the four began to discuss their plans. Gigi told them about Jarvis's idea to use the lifter.

"How did they get her in here?" Gigi asked.

"I think they had to cut a wall out of her house and use a crane," Elaine answered her, noting the surprised looks on their faces.

Clarissa continued the account, "And, then, they had to use a special gurney and a special ambulance to transport her. Mickey told me that it took five guys to get her into the ambulance."

"How much does she weigh now?" Cathy whispered.

"I don't know exactly," Clarissa spoke in a hushed tone, "but, we can check the scale at the foot of her bed when we go in."

"Here comes Jarvis now," Gigi said, looking up.

Jarvis stealthily pushed the Hoyer lifter, a large metal contraption, to the room. The arms at the base were in a closed position, and at the back, Jarvis guided it by the tall metal mast from which protruded the boom for lifting, secured into the mast sleeve at the base. Suspended from the boom was the free-swinging cradle onto which the sling would be hooked. Jarvis steadied the cradle with one hand as he steered the lifter, rolling it easily on its solid black casters.

As he approached the small group, Cathy noted that a digital scale was located on the mast near the battery pack. She saw his hand on the cradle and wondered if there were a sling large enough to accommodate Miss Epperson.

"What is the weight limit on this lift, Jarvis?" Clarissa asked.

"I think it goes up to five hundred pounds."

"Then, it won't lift her," Elaine added, "What are we going to do now?"

"Why don't we do this," he suggested, "I'll try to pull her from the front and Cathy and Gigi can push from the back...just enough so you can get the sling under her. We won't use it to lift her; we'll just pull her up."

"And then, while we've got her up, Elaine and I can start changing her bedding," Clarissa offered.

"Sounds like a plan," Jarvis whispered back.

"Jarvis, we can probably get the sling under her, but how will we get it out from the other side? I don't think that it will be wide enough," Elaine informed him.

"She's right," Cathy added, "If we don't do this correctly, we could hurt her. I really don't know what to do."

"Just do what you can," Hazel joined the group. "We want to accomplish this and preserve as much of Miss Epperson's dignity as we can. This will prove to be pretty embarrassing for her." As charge nurse, the orders were Hazel's call and she knew that the others would comply. "And, that goes for you, too, Georgina. I don't want to hear any catty remarks once we enter that room."

"Whatever," Gigi said under her breath, nodding as she seethed. With Hazel's spoken word, the group entered the dimly lit room, donned latex gloves, and took their places around Miss Epperson's bed.

"Miss Epperson," Clarissa began, "How are you doing today?"

"Well," she retorted, "I'm still fat."

Cathy found amazement in the woman's sense of humor, but Gigi stood beside her smiling wryly, shaking her head. Miss Epperson spoke lightheartedly of her plight, despite the fact that her voluminous mass covered most of her bed.

If not but for the grace of God ran through Cathy's mind while Jarvis explained the procedure at hand. Cathy knew that once they were finished, she and Gigi would return to their patients, to their lives, and to their homes, but Miss Epperson would still be trapped in her body; a body that should have been serving her to accomplish her hopes and dreams. Instead, it had become a prison of her own making, preventing her from performing even the simplest tasks to care for herself, enslaving her to its voracious appetite. Being totally dependent on others, Miss Epperson understood the difficulty, and said that she would cooperate with them in any way that she could.

"My options are rather limited," she said, grinning. When she smiled, her eyes, which had first appeared as tiny blue dots, disappeared into her face. Her once-pretty red hair had been cut off, but had begun to grow out again. Cathy didn't mean to stare, but she was overwhelmed with the sight of Miss Epperson. Her pale skin was stretched and riddled with sores, denied for years, the light of day. Never before had Cathy seen such obesity; the overflowing rolling of flesh.

Very little about her was in proper order, and when

she noticed Cathy's blank expression, she blushed and quickly excused herself and her appearance. Cathy gently patted her hand and did her best to straighten the sheet to cover her, while Elaine carefully untangled the tubes of the catheter bag and moved it to the foot of the bed. As she straightened the bag, Cathy saw her push the buttons on the bed scale.

After fully explaining what they were going to do, Jarvis maneuvered the lifter into position, and Gigi and Cathy waited to do as they were told. He gently straightened Miss Epperson's oxygen tubes before raising the rail back in place on his side of her bed. As Elaine lowered the bed rail on the other side, she whispered in Cathy's ear, "Six eleven," as Gigi took her place behind Miss Epperson's shoulders. Cathy was positioned at her buttocks.

Elaine stood between Cathy and Gigi, and on the count of "three," they all pushed and Jarvis pulled, raising Miss Epperson just enough so that Clarissa could begin sliding the sling in under her, down the length of her body. She had to work quickly, for the others could not hold her in position for an extended length of time.

When the sling was finally in place, Gigi, Elaine, and Cathy all ran their hands in under Miss Epperson to push it as far under her as they could get it. When they were finished, Jarvis lowered the cradle of the lifter and hooked the grommets of the sling onto it. Slowly, he pumped the hydraulic lever with his foot, and gently the cradle of the lifter began to rise. Not being centered on the sling, only the right side of Miss Epperson's body was rising, and the four began to push her toward Jarvis as Miss Epperson held on to the bed rail.

When she was fully on her side, Cathy heard the hydraulics of the lifter groan under her weight, and even though the top sheet had slid off of Miss Epperson's body, Cathy had no choice but to maintain her position at Miss Epperson's backside, while Gigi held her stance behind her shoulders. Clarissa began removing the soiled bedding at the head of the bed, while Elaine worked at the foot, rolling the linens lengthwise, and pushing them as far up under the sling as they could go.

Miss Epperson's backside was the largest that Cathy had ever seen, and she thought it incredible that she could not tell where the cheeks of her buttocks ended and the tops of her thighs began. Bent and squared with her arms extended, she pushed with all of her might with her arms and, at times, the top of her head, against Miss Epperson's right butt cheek, so that Elaine could work freely. Gigi positioned herself accordingly behind Miss Epperson's shoulders, allowing Clarissa greater access to place clean linens on that side of the bed.

Then it happened: that invisible cloud of noxious gas that came spewing forth from Miss Epperson's bowels. Immediately recognizing the sound, Elaine dove below Cathy for cover, while Cathy held her stance against the full impact of the onslaught. Her head also lowered, Gigi stood with outstretched arms and tightly pursed her lips, stifling the laughter that was trying to burst forth from her chest. All Cathy could do was to try to hold her breath, which really did no good at all.

Her arms locked in position, Cathy continued to push against the weight, despite the burning ache in her muscles. Her arms trembled, and she feared her elbows would buckle and her stomach felt nauseous as the acrid vapors overtook her.

Miss Epperson began to profusely apologize, and Clarissa stroked her face, reassuring her that everything was all right. When the linens were in place on Cathy's side of the bed, Jarvis finally gave Clarissa a signal to raise the bed rail, and he gently lowered Miss Epperson's body.

Cathy quickly backed out of the door where, in the hallway, she could discreetly inhale fresh air. She felt weakened and leaned against the wall as she gulped, unaware of the aching in her arms and her back. Elaine momentarily checked on her, letting her know that they were ready to repeat the procedure on the other side of the bed.

She could only imagine Miss Epperson's embarrassment, so she came smiling into the room, inquiring of Miss Epperson if she were doing all right. Gigi hurriedly took her place behind Miss Epperson's shoulders, and once again, Cathy found herself staring into the crevice of the formidable backside. This time, however, she had decided that she would turn her head while maintaining her stance.

The second part of the procedure seemed to go more smoothly than the former, as everyone knew what to expect, but the task was far from easy. However, it wasn't long before the groaning of the hydraulics ceased, and Miss Epperson was positioned comfortably. The four met in the hallway where they discussed what they had just experienced.

Gigi leaned against the wall with her head lowered so the others could not see that she was on the verge of laughter. Clarissa was shaking her head, muttering, "Lordy," under her breath.

"Well, that's something you definitely don't see every day," Elaine chuckled.

"Shh," Cathy cautioned, as Hazel and Jarvis exited the patient's room.

"Thank you, girls," Hazel said, "Now, let's all get back to our stations.

"I need to stop by the locker room first," Cathy said, "Then, I'll be back to finish up...if that's okay."

"That's all right," the charge nurse answered, "Georgina can cover for you until you get back."

Clarissa thanked Cathy and Gigi for their help, and she and Elaine returned to their workstation. Gigi followed Cathy hastily up the hallway to the employee locker room.

Once inside the door, the laughter that Gigi had held in for so long burst forth. As Cathy stood at the sink washing her face, amid the running water and the scrubbing, she could faintly hear, "I'm sorry, Cat. I'm sorry, Cat," strangled by Gigi's immutable laughter.

CHAPTER 7

As for Shepherd-of-the-Hills, the remainder of the day was as Cathy had expected; the diary did have to wait until she got home. It's just as well, she thought, Harry and the kids will be gone and I can get ready for bed early and kick back and read.

"See you Monday, Gigi," Cathy said as they strolled across the parking lot, inhaling the crisp evening air.

"What are you doing for dinner?" her friend inquired.

"Chinese. I'll stop on the way home."

"Why don't you come and eat dinner with Fred and me? We're not doing anything tonight."

"Naw, it's rare that I get the house to myself these days," she lied, "and besides, I haven't had Chinese in quite a while and I just want to crash early."

"Okay. Call me if you need anything," Gigi entreated over her shoulder, her hair flouncing as she made her way to her car.

As her car was warming, Cathy scrolled through her address book on her cell phone for the number of Peng's Pagoda. After calling in her dinner order, she made her way stealthily out of the parking lot and negotiated the rush hour traffic. Before she knew it, she had reached the ridge cut and was only minutes away from picking up her dinner.

Peng had her order waiting for her when she arrived. They exchanged pleasantries and Cathy stepped out into the cold, feeling a bit lonesome...a bit lost. It might not have been a nice feeling, but at least, it was familiar.

Darkness had descended and the night was colder by the time Cathy had arrived home. Harry was on the road, *somewhere,* and Michael and Heather were gone, *somewhere,* too. Cathy felt as though she were *nowhere.* The warmth of her house seemed to lighten her somber mood.

Her plan was simplicity, itself. Maybe this won't be so bad, she thought as she placed her dinner on the computer table in her bedroom and pressed the button on her computer until the circular blue light flashed. While the computer was booting up, she searched around the unmade bed until she found the remote to turn on the television.

Goose bumps undulated on her flesh as she stripped off her clothes and quickly showered. She put on fresh night clothes and sat down at her computer to eat dinner; her usual place when her husband was out of town. Her e-mail revealed a sweet "I Love You" from Harry and she knew that he would call her before she went to sleep.

Her hunger was satiated with a feast of Moo Goo Gai Pan and Egg Drop soup as she played computer games and watched television. Time and solitude helped her to unwind. Sitting cross-legged in her chair with the sumptuous dish before her, her chopsticks clicked as she ate while becoming engrossed in a movie.

Michael came in around nine o'clock to get ready to go out again. They were all going to a Halloween haunted house on Lookout Mountain, she had heard

Heather say. He and Cathy had grown apart since he had become a teenager. They had nothing in common and she found it difficult to get him to talk to her. Harry was quite close to him, though, and Cathy felt useless in Michael's life. However, he came in and kissed her cheek before he left, and she was taken aback; quite surprised and appreciative. Heather called shortly thereafter to tell her that she would be spending the night at Angela's. Cathy was not at all surprised. Her children had outgrown her; they had lives of their own.

Her expected phone call from Harry, who had almost reached St. Louis, came shortly before ten o'clock when he was stopping for the night. Cathy could tell that he was tired and did not keep him on the phone long. With a promise to call him tomorrow, she kissed him, once more, good night over the phone. She continued, for some time, playing computer games and watching television for the next couple of hours.

Tired of sitting in her chair, Cathy went to the kitchen and prepared a midnight sweet snack and retired to her bedroom. Reducing the volume on the television, she positioned herself, comfortably, in her bed, careful not to upset the bed tray, and lit a cigarette. Her gaze wandered to her bedroom window, but there was no use to look out; it was too dark to see anything. The early night's stiff breeze had changed its tone and now whipped about fiercely as a wind, howling lowly and menacingly. The diary on the nightstand beckoned her.

Events of the day tumbled through her mind and she found herself to be discontented. Her discontent bordered on anger, anger at the day, anger at the night, anger at Life, itself. Change your thoughts! Change your thoughts! she shouted to herself. Taking a deep breath,

Cathy closed her eyes and momentarily expelled all of her thoughts and sat in the vast, untimely blackness of her subconscious

Nothing. Nothing. Such a good nothing.

Suddenly, she found herself staring at strange wallpaper of greens and browns, distorted in the lamplight. A tide of warm feeling washed over her, physically perceptible, as she listened to a storm that raged outside. The sofa upon which she was sitting was large and brown, and hard and soft, all at the same time. From her perspective, she could see out the front window during flashes of lightning, a box elder flailing its arms wildly in the wind, and the elms bent to the wind's will, as their leaves were being torn from their grasps. A lonely figure rocked slowly, back and forth, back and forth, in front of the fire that had crept back under the logs and had hidden in the embers.

Very carefully, the resident bent forward and picked up the fireplace poker. Pursing her lips, she stoked the fire, forcing the little blaze from its hiding place. The flames licked the sides of the logs until the room illuminated, if only for a moment. Cathy held her breath, keeping her mouth tightly closed.

The woman's emotions were simple and direct. Fear and loneliness and tears. No doubt, she had been pondering at what point in her life she had become wholly mature, as well as, wholly corrupt, her battle of redemption still before her. Cathy did not understand and wondered how she knew these things. Without warning, the woman turned her head and faced Cathy, mouthing words that Cathy could not make out. Suddenly, the words, "The Blood of the Lamb, Jesus, shelter me," entered her mind and she felt soothed in the presence of the storm.

* * *

The images dismissed themselves rapidly, and Cathy leaned back against her pillows, shaking her head briskly. "The Blood of the Lamb," she said, aloud, "Jesus, shelter me." A comforting sensation filled her and she smiled for no reason, though she still did not fully understand what she had just *seen.*

Unable to make sense of the images, she glanced at her bedside table to the diary, musing as to any connection. She noticed that her restlessness and discontent had dissipated, and her head seemed very clear.

She felt strangely relaxed and able to concentrate and decided that now was the time that she could continue to read, uninterrupted. Besides, the diary would have to be dealt with before she could return to her project in the garage. Midnight did not concern her for she could sleep in tomorrow. The aged tome was opened with caution, so as not to rend any of the pages.

Friday, January 28, 1938

This is a beautiful day. The water finally came on about one o'clock. So I did my washing this afternoon and ironed more than half of them tonight.

I think Mable went to the Roosevelt Ball tonight at the grammar school building. Ned and Ravanell are in the sitting room. Charles is out playing. Judge is not in so good a mood. He does not seem to be feeling well today. I have been too busy to pay much attention.

Saturday, January 29, 1938

Just the usual Saturday routine.

Sunday, January 30, 1938

To S.S. and church as usual. Quite a large crowd attended. No services at either of the churches. Got a taxi and went up home this afternoon. Madge went too. Baby brought me back. Oliver stayed with Judge tonight while I went to church. The services were the young people from the three churches at the Baptist church.

Cathy mused again about the name, Judge, and wondered if it were a name or an occupation. *This must be Lynette's employer. But, who is Baby?* The questions were bricks stacking into a wall that only the elusive answers could tear down. However, she did not know that the value of her intentions would prove to be the cornerstone of her search.

Monday, January 31, 1938

It is real cold again. Nothing special today I believe.

Cathy got up to go to the bathroom and then to the kitchen for another soda. She had finished reading the month of January and hoped that it would get more interesting or she would be tempted to go to sleep.

The naked tree branches outside her bedroom window were rattling skeletons as the night wind of October howled through them. The sound sent chills up her spine. Settling herself back in her bed, she lit another cigarette and opened the diary to February 1. *Why did you hide this diary, Lynette?*

CHAPTER 8

Tuesday, February 1, 1938

To the doctor this morning. Dr. Warrenfells told me I should not have a baby for another year.

Took Aunt Ellen to the dentist this afternoon. Dr. Winslow took out four teeth. She'll soon have them all out and have some new ones.

Cathy furiously wrote these new bits of information. She postulated that Lynette was not an older woman. *She must have recently lost a baby, but who is her husband?* Cathy pondered in silence the growing list of questions which had drawn out into a prolonged sigh. Still, she needed to know more.

Clue by clue, she hoped to find, in the aggregate, a complete picture of common life in the thirties. The hour was growing later, but getting her second wind, she decided to read until she had gleaned enough information to satisfy her curiosity. *Why am I so curious? What has put this longing in my heart to seek to put the puzzle pieces together, to not rest until I have found the solution to something unsolved?*

Wednesday, February 2, 1938

Went to P.T.A. meeting this afternoon.

Thursday, February 3, 1938

Nowhere today except out to see Miss Mary Lizzie. I go there almost every afternoon. I enjoy reading with her the Spiritual Meditation in My Utmost for His Highest by Dr. Oswald Helton.

Friday, February 4, 1938

Papa's birthday. No school this afternoon because of a teachers' meeting so I had early dinner and Charles and I went up home on the twelve o'clock bus. Maude was there. They were just ready to eat dinner so we ate again. Baby took Maude to the train then brought me to LaFayette.

At last! Finally, the town! LaFayette. LaFayette, Georgia, Cathy wrote in her notebook. She knew where LaFayette was, as it was not far from Chattanooga. A small comfortable, southern town, LaFayette was nestled in one of the most beautiful areas that Georgia had to offer, a source of pride and inspiration. It offered contemporary life styles to its residents, while insulating them from the ravages of the outside world.

She and Harry had been through the area several times on their way to Summerville, stopping at junk shops and a flea market on the way. Once, they had eaten lunch at the Sunrise Cafe, a small eatery on the town square, where colorful murals depicting the town's history covered all of the walls. LaFayette offered a slower pace and breathing room.

Saturday, February 5, 1938

To Miss Mary Lizzie's this afternoon.

Sunday, February 6, 1938

To S.S. and church. To Miss Mary Lizzie's this afternoon. To church tonight. Charles went to Junior League, but did not go to church.

Sadie came awhile. Mrs. Burton is teaching our class for awhile.

Monday, February 7, 1938

I stayed quite awhile over at Miss Mary Lizzie's this morning. Did not feel like doing anything so I just stayed over there. Went to Missionary meeting this afternoon.

Tuesday, February 8, 1938

Had a card from Baby last night. She said Aunt Ellen is there and will be down here tomorrow so I did my washing today. And got the ironing all done tonight.

Wednesday, February 9, 1938

Aunt Ellen came with Baby this morning. She will stay a day or two with me. I went to the dentist with her this afternoon. Dr. Winslow extracted six teeth for her. She will be back in a few more weeks for him to make a plate for her.

I did not go to Prayer meeting tonight.

Thursday, February 10, 1938

Aunt Ellen is feeling better today. But I told her to wait until tomorrow to go home. So she just sat around and crocheted nearly all day. She is trying to learn a new pattern.

Friday, February 11, 1938

I had early dinner today and went with Aunt Ellen to the bus which leaves here at twelve o'clock but it was late and I came on home before it came.

I went to see Dr. Warrenfells this afternoon. I was not so nervous as I was last week.

Saturday, February 12, 1938

Judge walked up to the barber shop this morning. The first time he has been out in several weeks.

Sunday, February, 13, 1938

To S.S. and church. Mrs. Burton taught the class.

Cooked dinner before I went to S.S. As soon as I got through with dinner Sara and Ravanell took Charles and me up home. Judge went too but he came back with the girls. Helen and William were there. They brought me home. Charles and Kerry Fox walked to Rock Spring. To church tonight.

Monday, February 14, 1938

Brother Cash came this afternoon. Mr. Grubb, the postman, brought me a letter today from [C!] A beautiful valentine. I thought he might have forgotten. Judge did. He wanted to know when he could come over so I looked around for chores to be done. I was glad for I know he is worth it.

Who is Judge and who is [C!]? Cathy thought. *If Lynette were domestic help, then why would she expect Judge to remember Valentine's Day? And how does [C!] figure into the picture?* She sensed a possible "back stairs" romance developing, probably at Judge's chagrin. Cathy knew that she would feel better about this undertaking if she could untangle the steadily growing list of players. The thought never crossed her mind that she might never know, and she concluded to reserve her judgment until she had completed the diary. More mystery, yet the diary yielded few context clues to guide her thinking.

Cathy noted Lynette's visits to the doctor and her feelings for [C!] and Judge, and she was much more perplexed than ever. In the thirties, drug addiction was heard of only in "the big city," where dope fiends found narcotics to be plentiful. In small towns, however, the stigma was removed from a narcotics addiction if the 'fix' were administered by a licensed physician. It seemed to Cathy that Lynette's visits to Dr. Warrenfells indicated that she had been, indeed, addicted to something. She felt as though she were prying into private matters now, but she could not help herself, so she kept on reading.

Tuesday, February 15, 1938

Nothing special today. Just the daily routine. Went to Miss Mary Lizzie's and left a note for [C!] under the milk can on the back porch. Then to town.

Wednesday, February 16, 1938

Baby came as usual this morning. I could hear her singing "Go Tell Aunt Rhody" as she came up the back steps.

Washed today. Ravanell did not go to school. To Prayer meeting tonight.

This reference to Baby told Cathy that Baby was not a child, but an adult who came to Lynette's on a frequent basis. Perhaps, Baby was a friend or a neighbor, who dropped by now and then for coffee, and Cathy wondered how she came to bear the nickname, "Baby." She had been important enough for Lynette to include her quite frequently, so now, she had to reason it out. She hoped that Baby would not turn out to be a local oddity.

The diary, thus far, had proved to be somewhat of a disappointment. However, Cathy had wanted adventure, and just because the adventure was not what she had expected, was no reason to throw it back in God's face. Sometimes, the unusual undertaking was breathtaking and exciting, and sometimes, the curious undertaking was not; and this one seemed to fall into the category of the latter. So, she decided to make the best of it and to see it through to the end.

Thursday, February 17, 1938

Baked a cocoanut cake today and dressed a hen. So that much of my Sunday's dinner is finished.

To Miss Mary Lizzie's this afternoon. Mrs. Coulter was there so I didn't get to check under the milk can.

Friday, February 18, 1938

To Miss Mary Lizzie's this afternoon for a little while. My reading was not favorable and Miss Mary Lizzie warned me to be careful. Nothing under the milk can.

Cathy imagined Miss Mary Lizzie to be an old woman, reading fortunes from tarot cards behind closed doors. Perhaps, she had been a practitioner of the Old Ways, and had spent her days preparing herbal potions and homemade remedies, and advising her neighbors on different aspects of their lives by interpreting Nature's signs and omens. She wrote down the words "fortune teller?" next to Miss Mary Lizzie's name, and wondered what Lynette's reading had foretold. *Milk can?*

Saturday, February 19, 1938

I asked Hattie and her family and

Madge and her family to have dinner with us tomorrow, but Madge called this morning, said Carl was not well enough to come and she was most afraid to bring Betty June out. She is just getting well of measles.

Sunday, February 20, 1938

To S.S. and church this morning. Mable and Charles went with Helen to Ringgold this afternoon. Nell and Sara were out somewhere.

Madge ate dinner with us but left just after dinner. Judge was in bed so I read. The afternoon passed all too soon. Want to go to church tonight, but Judge does not want me to go.

"Ringgold, Georgia," Cathy wrote, consulting her mental map. She had been through the town in Catoosa County, Georgia, just south of Chattanooga. LaFayette was in Walker County, northwest of Catoosa, and Cathy felt the presentiment of a road trip in her near future.

Monday, February 21, 1938

A nice fair day. I wanted to go see Dr. Warrenfells this afternoon because of my headache but Judge said he was not feeling well and did not want me to leave him alone.

Tuesday, February 22, 1938

A rainy day. Judge is better. I intended

to go to see Dr. Warrenfells even if it is raining, but Mable went over to Hattie Winslow's and I could not leave Judge alone though he is some better.

Wednesday, February 23, 1938

Well again I did not get to go see Dr. Warrenfells. It is cloudy and colder and I was tired after washing and was afraid that I would take cold—the influenza. Baby told me this morning that Maude is having to take the Pasteur Treatment. Charles and I went to Prayer meeting tonight.

Thursday, February 24, 1938

Went to Dr. Warrenfells this afternoon. There was no pain at all except the needle in my arm and it hurt but not so I couldn't stand it.

I baked my cakes this morning for Sunday's dinner.

Friday, February 25, 1938

Charles went to Frances Hammond's birthday party this afternoon. I'm sure he had a good time.

I dressed my hen today for Sunday dinner. Hattie's folks are coming.

The little notebook's pages were filling: Maude—Pasteur Treatment; Lynette getting shots at the doctor for something. Cathy grouped the puzzle pieces, trying to make sense out of them. She reached into the nightstand drawer for another pack of cigarettes, opened it, and lit another before continuing.

Saturday, February 26, 1938

I never accomplish much on Saturday; I just do a little here and there. It is hard to concentrate when [C!] is here. He fixed the faucet.

Charles went to the show this afternoon. Judge is in his study.

Sunday, February 27, 1938

My company came today. Had a very good dinner. Everyone seemed to enjoy the day. I surely did. Those here for dinner were Hattie, Dr. and Mrs. Winslow, Carl and Madge and Betty June, and Oliver and Lee. Helen and William came in the afternoon. [C!] came in the afternoon to finish the faucet. He would not come for dinner. Judge and I took K.C.F. back down to Lucile's mother's in the afternoon. Mary Louise has measles. To church tonight.

Monday, February 28, 1938

To the Circle meeting this afternoon at Mrs. Hosick's. Judge is in a particularly foul mood.

Tuesday, March 1, 1938

Mable and Hattie went to Chattanooga

today. I had planned to have dinner early and take the twelve o'clock bus to go up home. Judge is feeling very well and I went on anyway even if Mable was gone. Charles got his dinner up in town. Papa and Baby were getting ready to come to L—so we came on back down here.

Feeling a surge of excitement, Cathy felt as though she had found another piece of the puzzle. *Papa and Baby. Baby must be her sister!* She could feel the sense of family around Lynette and her existence now seemed more humane. Cathy could now visualize Lynette's mounting frustration and apprehension, and she could feel her blood course through her veins.

Wednesday, March 2, 1938

Went to P.T.A. meeting this afternoon.

Thursday, March 3, 1938

Nothing special today I believe. Miss Mary Lizzie gave me a reading and I found a note from [C!].

Friday, March 4, 1938

Nothing special today. Mable and Hattie went to Chattanooga tonight. Mable is headstrong and likes to have a good time. She will not listen. If she's not careful Ravanell will have a little sister.

These new developments whirled through Cathy's head. *So, Ravanell is Mable's daughter. How old are these people?* Cathy shook her head in aggravation. Without meaning to, she had formulated ideas about these characters, and she found it inconsiderate of them not to pigeonhole themselves as she had imagined them. Now, her thinking must begin anew. Let the characters tell you where they belong, she instructed herself.

Saturday, March 5, 1938

Just the ordinary routine today. Mable and Hattie went out again tonight. Ravanell is spending too much time with Ned. I tried to talk to Mable about it but she was in a hurry to leave with Hattie. She could be a grandmother at 34 and I can't even be a mother at 28.

Wow! This is major! Cathy mused. *Lynette is only 28 years old, so she must be a domestic working for the judge. Perhaps, Mable is his daughter and his granddaughter has to be Ravanell! But, who is Charles?*

Sunday, March 6, 1938

To S.S. and church this morning. Sara S. ate dinner with us today and took Charles and me up home when I got through with the dishes.

Tom, Maude and the children were there this afternoon. He took pictures this afternoon. One of Maude, Baby, and me standing around Papa's chair. I enjoyed being with them so much. Baby brought us back to L—in her milk truck. Charles and I went to church tonight.

Cathy turned the pages of the diary carefully, as she

thought about the picture that was taken of Maude, Lynette, and Baby around Papa's chair. It seemed that Maude and Baby were Lynette's sisters, so Cathy wrote this information in her little notebook and circled the names. Next to [C!] she wrote the word "boyfriend."

Monday, March 7, 1938

To the Missionary Society this afternoon at Mrs. Hosick's.

Tuesday, March 8, 1938

Have not been feeling very well today. Seem to be taking cold but will try to break it up. No word from [C!].

Wednesday, March 9, 1938

To Prayer meeting tonight. Hattie, Lucile and Emily were there.

Thursday, March 10, 1938

I ironed and cleaned up the house today. Ravanell and Ned are pretty thick these days.

Friday, March 11, 1938

Gentle Lee Inman was buried this afternoon. The influenza. Mable went to the funeral. I baked an angel food cake to take to the family this morning.

Saturday, March 12, 1938

I heard Baby's beautiful voice as usual this morning. My butter and eggs are blooming, but others beat me to them.

The odd phrase perplexed Cathy. *Butter and eggs are blooming? Must be a local expression,* she decided. She added Gentle Lee Inman's name to the Hosick Funeral Home list.

Sunday, March 13, 1938

To S.S. and church today. Sara S. ate dinner with us. Did not go anywhere this afternoon except to Miss Mary Lizzie's.

Went to church tonight. Mable spent the night with Lucile. [C!] has taken Kerry and Seab and Jimmy to Warm Springs.

Cathy formulated the opinion that [C!] was married to Lucile, and Kerry, Seab, and Jimmy must be his children, and felt embarrassment at invading their privacy. Now, she knew that Lynette was in love with a married man, and she felt ashamed that now she was reading to find out about the scandal.

Cathy began to feel sorry for Lynette, a woman she felt, had found herself in such a socially unacceptable, if not desperate, situation...a love triangle. Yet, in the eyes of her neighbors, her predominant routine was religion, and each day held its religious significance for her. Such confidential information had not been written for others to read, but she could not stop herself.

Finding no comfort in this last thought, Cathy arose, filled with an overwhelming restlessness. Her mouth was dry, so she strolled to the kitchen for another soda. As she passed Michael's room, she noticed that he was already in for the night, and it surprised her that she had been so engrossed in what she had been reading that she had not heard him come in.

She had even been totally unaware of the shrieking of the storm, the wind shaking the house with a great force and regularity. However, no matter how fierce the wind wailed, it could not penetrate the security of the Billings' abode. The storm had no choice but to rail through the trees until it blew itself out in the early morning hours.

Chapter 9

Monday, March 14, 1938

Squire Brown came to see Judge this afternoon. Went over to Miss Mary Lizzie's this afternoon. Also to see Mrs. Hosick.

Mable has gone to the Mission study course tonight, or so she says. She spent the night again with Lucile. I wish [C!] would come home.

Tuesday, March 15, 1938

Went to town this afternoon. Bought material to make me two dresses and two slips. Began one of the slips this afternoon. Again Mable stayed with Lucile.

Wednesday, March 16, 1938

[C!] and the boys got home today. Lucile and the children ate supper with us tonight, but he would not come. Mable helped me cook supper.

Sibyl Deck ran to see me just a few minutes this afternoon. Oliver and Lee, Helen and William were all here with Mable and Lucile.

Thursday, March 17, 1938

Charles went to the American Legion Auxiliary meeting this afternoon at Mrs. LaFollette Hammond's. Mrs. Rhyne has organized an orchestra of her violin pupils. So Charles played in the orchestra there.

Mable and Hattie went shopping in Chattanooga today in Hattie's new automobile.

Friday, March 18, 1938

The children did not have to go to school this afternoon because of a teachers' meeting. Charles had a good time playing all afternoon with Kerry Fox.

Saturday, March 19, 1938

Has rained all afternoon. Mable went down to Lucile's early tonight. I wonder if she knows, but she makes no sign of it. Ravanell is out with Ned. Judge, Charles and I are alone. Did not go to Miss Mary Lizzie's at all today.

Baby said that Tom and Maude, Mildred and Mary spent the day with her Thursday.

Sunday, March 20, 1938

Carl and Madge spent the day with me. I enjoyed having them very much. The baby is so very sweet, much like I imagine my little Markie would have been had she lived, and much like my little Sammy who is now one of God's angels in Heaven. I went to S.S. but did not go to church. They came about eleven.

Mable went home with Hattie from S.S. and did not come in until late this afternoon. Judge does not like it that she stays gone so long and often and he lets us all know it. Judge did not let me go to church tonight. He said he wasn't feeling well.

Iva June Burton was found dead this morning. The influenza.

Bits and pieces of seventy-year-old information about Lynette sparked Cathy's interest even further. Lynette, a twenty-eight-year-old woman, had lost two children, so she must have been married back in 1938, but to whom? *Judge could be her husband.* Cathy mused. *Or maybe she's his nurse because he treats her like hired help. But, who is [C!], and is he really married to Lucile?* Now, Cathy was determined to find out more about this woman she did not know.

Monday, March 21, 1938

[C!] took Jimmy, Kerry, Seab and Charles to Cloudland with the Boy

Scouts so Mable is again staying with Lucile at night. They went to Chattanooga today. I went to see Dr. Warrenfells this afternoon. We decided that I would have one more shot for my headaches and he gave me some powder to take home.

Mrs. Hosick and I went to see Mrs. Dunwoody this afternoon. She is quite sick. Lucile and Mable were here until about bed time tonight. Judge was angry today. He can be so cruel sometimes.

Tuesday, March 22, 1938

Mable went to Lucile's again tonight, but [C!] and the boys will be home tomorrow night. The Boy Scouts are going to see the Holy Land exhibit at Warner Park. I will be glad to see Charles and Kerry.

Wednesday, March 23, 1938

Charles got home early in the afternoon so we went to Prayer meeting tonight. Judge would not let me go by myself. Judge looks at me as though he is on the verge of accusing me of something.

Thursday, March 24, 1938

Charles went to the Music Club at Mrs. Massey's.

Friday, March 25, 1938

A pretty day. Miss Mary Lizzie doesn't seem to be so well today. Charles went to the show tonight. Judge and I drank cocoa in the sitting room.

Saturday, March 26, 1938

Charles went to Betty Allen's party this afternoon. He had a good time. Everyone gone tonight except Judge and me. Charles is out at Walter's. He will be in directly.

Sunday, March 27, 1938

To S.S. and church today. Walter Cobb went with Charles and me up home this afternoon. I got Sara to take us. Baby brought us back. Went to church tonight.

Monday, March 28, 1938

Aunt Ellen came this morning. She went to the dentist this afternoon. I went to the Circle meeting at Julianna Rhyne's.

Tuesday, March 29, 1938

Aunt Ellen made a dress for Baby today. She also went to Dr. Winslow's to have her teeth fitted at eleven. I did not go with her because I was busy cooking dinner and I could not leave Judge alone.

Wednesday, March 30, 1938

I did the washing today even if Aunt Ellen was here. I also went with her to see Dr. Winslow at 10:30. Got back something after eleven finished dinner so she could eat then I went with her to the bus at twelve. Judge was glad to see her go and let me know about it later when I got back. Finished the washing then rested. My clothes dried real well today. Mable and Hattie went to Chattanooga today.

Thursday, March 31, 1938

Then I did my ironing today. Judge was not in a good state of mind and he eyes me suspiciously. I tried to stay out of his way but he followed me from room to room as I did my chores. I finally fixed him some cocoa and put him to bed.

Friday, April 1, 1938

April Fool's Day. I cleaned up the house today. Then went over to Miss Mary Lizzie's. She slept all afternoon while [C!] cleaned up the yard. I cannot describe the excitement that fills my soul when he holds me. It pains me to be near him and it pains me to be away from him. I love him so.

So! Lynette is in love with whoever [C!] is, and he's married to someone else, and she's married to someone else (probably Judge)! This is too good, Cathy thought, and suddenly felt pangs of shame. Her absorption into the drama was too much; she had to reread several passages to be sure about what she had read, as fatigue overtook her.

Her head dropped, her eyes closed, and she made an effort to open them, but gave in to the futility of the effort. It crossed her mind again and again that she had a problem with these invaders in her brain; that she needed to find out all that she could about them. She needed to know Lynette's values and about her duty to her family. Cathy knew too much here, too little there. Maude, Baby, and Papa, Ravanell and Ned, Mable and Hattie, and Charles, yes, Charles and Miss Mary Lizzie. [C!] and Lucile, Judge, Emily and Tommy, Oliver and Lee; to S.S. and church. These people came to her from nowhere, for some reason. Her uneasy sleep did not last long, and the minute she opened her eyes, she fumbled for her place in the diary.

Saturday, April 2, 1938

I helped Ravanell tonight—to fix some sandwiches tonight. She and Betty Allen and their boyfriends were here.

Mable is out somewhere.

Sunday, April 3, 1938

To S.S. and church today, but did not go anywhere this afternoon. To church tonight at the Baptist church. Went on up there to hear their new preacher, Mr. Story.

Monday, April 4, 1938

Should have received an anniversary present from Judge but I guess he forgot. We've been married eight years. Difficult years. Sometimes I wonder why I married him, but I guess I still love him.

Judge is haughty and so prides himself on his influence and power over others. He abuses his power and then claims to have treated people justly, as he did in his courtroom. He once even told me that he never knew a man, woman or child that could not be bought or sold like a bale of cotton. To the Missionary meeting this afternoon.

Bingo! The thought raced through Cathy's mind. She had been right in her assumption that Lynette was actually the judge's wife and she was seeing [C!] on the side, meeting him at Miss Mary Lizzie's house and exchanging notes under the milk can on Miss Mary Lizzie's back porch. Mable was Judge's daughter, and Ravanell was his granddaughter. She had not quite figured out Charles, but she hoped that bit of information would come soon.

She had always imagined that , a few decades ago, small town life had been inordinately boring, but now her opinion was changing. Still, she wondered how they had managed without cell phones, microwave ovens, automatic washers and dryers, fast food, television, and the Internet. Somehow, they had managed it, and had done so quite well. *Maybe you don't miss what you don't know.* But, she did reason that human nature was the same, despite the decade, and the same feelings and emotions that plagued and elated mankind today were well in effect back then, also. Times may change, but some things are still the same.

Cathy mentally painted imaginary scenarios of life in LaFayette in the thirties, and she made a concerted effort to understand that which was absolute back then, and was open to interpretation now. She concluded that most information of the day came to people by way of Mr. Grubb, the postman, the weekly newspaper, gossip, or by listening to news reports on the radio in the evening. Connected to the outside world by thin, invisible threads, this community went about its daily business, depending on God and each other.

Tuesday, April 5, 1938

Went to Dr. Warrenfells's this morning. I told him that the powder doesn't work as well as the shot. Afterwards, he told me to go home and lie down.

Wednesday, April 6, 1938

I did not go to the P.T.A. meeting this afternoon. I was too tired. Also it was raining. Miss Mary Lizzie gave me a reading this afternoon and was more bewildered than ever. She told me that the cards were strongly cautioning me about tragedy and she warned me to be extremely careful.

We were interrupted by Mrs. Hosick at the door. While they visited, I read a note from [C!] from under the milk can on the back porch. He says that he cannot wait until we can be together but it will be temporary as long as he and I belong to others. Went to Prayer meeting tonight. O God give me more strength. I fixed Judge some more cocoa.

Cathy found herself contemplating that even she, too, was grateful that Lynette had had Miss Mary Lizzie to turn to in time of need. Miss Mary Lizzie was believed to be the oldest woman in the county, who had spent most of her life in service to her neighbors: reading their cards, interpreting signs and omens, caring for them in sickness, and lifting them up in sorrow. She charged a nominal fee for reading, and it was not uncommon for her, in her placid state of mind, to foresee an illness somewhere, or a night's watching before her.

She taught Lynette about the Old Ways, and Lynette returned her favor by checking in on Miss Mary Lizzie every day, to see what she might need, or to share her company. Their friendship was solid, sturdy, and dependable, and they were always accessible to each other at a moment's notice, as their homes were situated only a stone's-throw apart on Mulberry Street.

Chapter 10

Thursday, April 7, 1938

Am up early this morning about 4:45 to read, study and pray.

Friday, April 8, 1938

I went to see Dr. Warrenfells about eleven o'clock.

Mable went to work at the courthouse today. Even though Judge retired three years ago, he still has influence.

Charles stayed all night with Walter Cobb tonight.

Saturday, April 9, 1938

It has been quite a disagreeable day. Judge is in a most foul frame of mind. I don't seem to be able to do anything to suit him.

I didn't go anywhere today, except to town and to Miss Mary Lizzie's. No word from [C!].

Sunday, April 10, 1938

To S.S. and church today. Ravanell and Sara ate dinner with Wallace and Mable today. Mable went for a ride with someone. Charles, Madge and I went up home this afternoon. Oliver was here awhile with Judge. To church tonight.

Monday, April 11, 1938

Did not go anywhere today except over to Miss Mary Lizzie's late this afternoon. She and I had the most wonderful time of practice and prayer.

Tuesday, April 12, 1938

Aunt Ellen got her new teeth this afternoon. She ate supper with them better than she thought she could. Think she will learn to wear them all right.

Brother Cash came this afternoon. All of us were here. He read the 34th Psalm and prayed.

Wednesday, April 13, 1938

To Prayer meeting tonight. The young people had charge of the service.

Thursday, April 14, 1938

Mary Louise Kremke is a corpse today. She suffered a heart attack and died last night. I went down there awhile this afternoon to help Lucile. Mrs. Lee and I stopped to see Mrs. Cash on our way back.

Friday, April 15, 1938

Miss Annie spent the day with Miss Mary Lizzie today. She went down to the school house and told the Easter story to the children. I went over to Miss Mary Lizzie's about twelve and after my reading we spent the day fasting and praying.

Saturday, April 16, 1938

The usual Saturday routine. [C!] stopped by to fix my washer. I can't explain how he makes me feel. My heart and my head won't agree.

Sunday, April 17, 1938

We had a very sweet Easter service today and again tonight. Mrs. Hosick took some photographs of Georgia Turner's baby, Florene, outside the church. Did not want to go anywhere this afternoon except to Miss Mary Lizzie's. I spent a few minutes with [C!]. Oliver and Perry were both here awhile.

Monday, April 18, 1938

Busy with the regular routine. Judge is still complaining so I fixed him another cup of cocoa.

Tuesday, April 19, 1938

Nothing special today. I wonder what [C!] is doing.

Wednesday, April 20, 1938

To prayer meeting tonight.

Thursday, April 21, 1938

Jimmy, Seab and Kerry spent the night with Charles tonight.

Rubbing her eyes, Cathy noticed that they felt gritty and painful. She went into the bathroom and washed her face, and the warm water seemed to soothe the stinging. Yawning, she repositioned herself on her pillows. *[C!] must be married to Lucille...and Jimmy, Seab and Kerry must be their children,* she reassured herself. *I wonder if Lucile ever found out about them. Maybe Judge found out about them and sentenced K.C. Fox to jail for some miniscule infraction. Something of great importance in her life must have happened for Lynette to retain the diary for all of these years and then to take such pains to hide it.*

Friday, April 22, 1938

Charles and Kerry went to the show this afternoon to see Tom Sawyer.

Saturday, April 23, 1938

Ravanell went somewhere this afternoon with Ned. Mrs. Kinsey came down tonight to fit my dress. It was very sweet of her to bring it down here. I hope [C!] likes it.

Mrs. Massey came over and sat with me awhile this afternoon. I was glad she came. Madge is a dear friend.

Sunday, April 24, 1938

Kerry and Seab ate dinner with Charles. Walter Cobb came after dinner and went with us up home. To Sunday School and church as usual. And to church tonight. Sara took us up home and Baby brought us back.

Monday, April 25, 1938

Circle No. One met with me this afternoon. It is so hard to sit there with Lucile and knowing that when she goes home she'll be with [C!]. I try to act interested in something else when she talks about him.

Tuesday, April 26, 1938

I went over to Miss Mary Lizzie's and met [C!]. Miss Mary Lizzie stayed in the house while we talked out back in the garden shed.

He is so handsome and his arms are so strong. I cannot refuse him when he holds me and kisses me and lies with me on the floor of the shed. O, God, forgive me for letting this man lift my skirt and lie with me. I've longed for him so. It feels good and bad all at the same time. Something I've never experienced with Judge. He told me that he loves me and wants to be with me, but he doesn't know how to tell Lucile. I feel so guilty.

Wednesday, April 27, 1938

Went to Prayer meeting tonight. I need to pray. I need to pray.

Thursday, April 28, 1938

I wanted to go to [C!]'s shop today but Judge would not let me go to town. I told him that the refrigerator has been acting up.

Friday, April 29, 1938

Mrs. Kinsey brought my dress to me this afternoon. I did not have the money to pay her and Judge did not want to pay her but he finally did.

Saturday, April 30, 1938

Charles went to Chattanooga on the bus today alone. He came back on the bus that leaves there at 5:45.

Hattie and Mable are out somewhere.

Sunday, May 1, 1938

To S.S. and church this morning. Willard and James Cash and Walter Cobb went with Charles and me up home this afternoon. The taxi took us up there and Baby brought us back. Mrs. Brown, their pastor's wife, was there.

Judge was sitting on the porch when we got back.

Monday, May 2, 1938

Baby and Maude came down this afternoon. I was so glad to see them. Maude came out there on the bus this morning. She got the 4:30 bus here to go back.

Tuesday, May 3, 1938

Shortened some of my clothes today.

Wednesday, May 4, 1938

This has been a very beautiful day. I got along fine with the washing. Washed a quilt also.

Went over to Miss Mary Lizzie's this afternoon. She had misplaced the key to her closet. We closed our eyes and prayed together and received a direct answer to prayer in finding it.

Thursday, May 5, 1938

It rained awfully hard early this morning, but it cleared up later in the day.

Friday, May 6, 1938

Charles went to the Confederacy this afternoon with Seab and Kerry. He has gone to the Senior play tonight. Ravanell is in it. The school was out at noon today because of a teachers' meeting. I have been nearly sick today. Brother Story came today to see Judge.

Saturday, May 7, 1938

Baby was here as usual this morning. The Apollo Boys' Choir is in LaFayette tonight. One of them spent the night with Charles. They had a picnic supper at the school house. Charles went to the concert too. The little boy who stayed here was David Charlton. I got awfully sleepy before they came in.

Sunday, May 8, 1938

To S.S. and church today. Sara came and got me to take me up home. Baby had an accident, she said. When she was doing the milking, a cow had stepped on Baby's foot. She didn't know if it was broken or not. As strong and husky as Baby is, the cow got the better of her. Her foot turned black.

Edsel and Georgia Turner took her to the Post hospital. Baby's foot is broken and Maude came over and said that she would stay with Baby tonight. Sara brought me out to Papa's. The neighbors were very kind. Had the milking done when I got there. I usually don't worry about Baby. She has always taken care of all of us. I cannot imagine life without her.

Monday, May 9, 1938

Mrs. Borders and Minnie came over and helped Charles and me milk this morning. Mr. and Mrs. Henry went to Chattanooga this morning so they went over and brought Baby home. Her foot is in a cast and has hurt all day, but she looks better than she did yesterday.

Sara came for me to take me to LaFayette this afternoon. Judge is aggravated at me not being there and he is not doing well at all.

Cathy wrote more in the notebook next to Baby's name: runs a milk route from somewhere to LaFayette. She must own a dairy farm. Something sounded vaguely familiar about this thought, but Cathy could not remember exactly where's she'd heard of it.

Tuesday, May 10, 1938

I had a card from Baby this morning, or rather afternoon. She said she is feeling much better today.

Dr. Warrenfells came this afternoon. He says Judge's heart is in a bad fix.

Wednesday, May 11, 1938

Baby came from Rock Spring this morning as usual. She looks bad and her foot hurts and she limps. Do hope she gets to feeling better soon.

Went to Prayer meeting tonight. Fixed some cocoa for Judge. Mable stayed with him while I was gone.

Evidently, Lynette's family is from Rock Spring, Cathy deduced, *and Baby runs a milk route, probably from the family dairy in Rock Spring to LaFayette. That's why she visits Lynette so much. And [C!] has to be K.C. Fox, the handyman who has a shop in town and is married to Lucile.* Cathy wrote feverishly in her notebook, trying to identify the characters and listing them with their family members.

Three distinct families were emerging from her categorized lists and suddenly, she seemed to begin to understand, but she didn't know how and she didn't know why. What she did know was that for some reason, the relationships of the individuals in the diary were beginning to make sense to her, and she could feel that she was on the right track.

The column on the left read:
Judge and Lynette
Mable (Sara S.)
Ravenell
Charles

The one in the center read:
Papa
Baby
Lynette
Maude

And the one on the right had the following names:

K.C. and Lucile Fox
Kerry, Seab, and Jimmy

Now, she could not let go. She had to find out where these people were and if any of them were still alive. She had already decided that when she finished the diary, she would make a trip to LaFayette to see what she could discover. The cosmos had handed her a dark mystery to investigate and a puzzle to be solved, for whatever reason. Not knowing disturbed her greatly, and her waking quest was now to satisfy her own curiosity.

Noises from the kitchen prompted her to look at the clock. The night was gone and morning stretched uneven fingers across the shadowy landscape and into her room. Michael was having breakfast before going to work at the shop, and Cathy felt groggy. She placed the diary on her nightstand and turned on her side, burying her head in between the pillows.

* * *

"Died in the millpond, Died in the millpond, Died in the millpond," echoed the eerie strains through the darkness of a cavernous wooden structure. Cathy raised up to see, in the light of the kerosene lamp, two silhouettes arguing in earnest. The larger of the two paced around what seemed to be a concrete floor strewn with hay, kicking against an iron rail at selected intervals; each kick a resounding thud. The other sat on a crate across from the rail, hunched over, crying uncontrollably.

Cathy slid her feet from under the covers and over the side of the bed, but could not find the floor. Suddenly the pacing figure ran to what appeared to be a stall, or tool room, and retrieved an axe. A high-pitched wail came from the woman sitting on the crate, as the axe came crashing down through the darkness, splattering blood across Cathy's face. Lost in a black void, Cathy had fallen backwards onto her bed, unable to see more, but able to hear the clanging of metal against metal.

Gripped with fear, she pulled her legs back up and under the covers, unable to speak. Suddenly, the cold heartless moon seemed to drift from behind darkened clouds, and its light shimmered on water. From her vantage point in her bed at the water's edge, she observed the water milfoil and yarrow, pulsating, rising and falling with the duckweed as tiny ripples undulated underneath before lapping the shore. Two silhouettes rowed silently to the middle of the water and as the darkened clouds returned to hide the nocturnal orb, Cathy could hear gurgling sounds amid muffled sobs.

* * *

"Mama! Mama!" a loud whisper permeated her consciousness. Attributing the voice to part of the dream, Cathy maintained her repose unresponsively.

"Mama!" the voice strained, and Cathy felt a gentle prod on her shoulder. Her first impulse was to shout and tell them, face to face, to get out and to go away and leave her alone.

When she opened her eyes, Heather was standing with a lunch tray at the side of her bed, whispering, "Mama!"

"Heather?" Cathy whispered, "What time is it?" Her eyes rapidly searched the room for rails and stalls, moonlight and water, and axes and blood. *That dream again! Boy, what a dream!*

"It's almost eleven," she answered, "I fixed you some lunch. Do you have five dollars?"

"What?"

"Do you have five dollars?" she queried again.

"Hand me my purse," Cathy said, sitting up in wakefulness. Heather carefully handed her the leather bag, and Cathy searched her wallet as her daughter waited patiently.

"It's okay if you don't," Heather said, setting the tray on Cathy's computer table. "Angie and I were going to the mall, and I wasn't really going to buy anything. I just wanted some lunch money."

"All I've got is a twenty," Cathy said, not fooled by her daughter's reticent manner. "Here, have fun."

"Thanks, Mom!" Heather grabbed Cathy around the neck and kissed her cheek. This is the way is always was: Heather was broke, very polite, very humble, and very appreciative when Cathy relinquished.

"Be careful, Heather," Cathy called.

"Love you, Mom," Heather called back as Cathy heard the slam of the front door.

Cathy got out of bed and looked at her lunch tray. There was hot tomato soup, bread and butter, corned beef hash, and a pear. She really didn't want it, but at least, Heather tried. The coffee was still warm, so she drank heartily and then lit a cigarette.

The day was gray and overcast, and she had no plans to go out this weekend. When she had finished the cup, she made her bed and then showered. In the kitchen, she found that the coffee in the pot was still hot, so another cup seemed to be in order. Sitting at her computer table in her robe while she smoked another cigarette, the mellow liquid was easily consumed. She checked her cell phone for a message from Harry, and having retrieved it, noticed that she had forgotten to charge the battery, so she plugged the charger into the bottom of her phone and proceeded to check her e-mail.

Cathy glanced at the diary on the nightstand. Beneath the surface of her mind, held there by some sort of control that she was not even conscious of sensing, was a turmoil of pain, despair, hurt, and chagrin. She felt a general foreboding about this stranger who had worked her way into her head, and now into her heart, as Cathy was now aware of an emotional investment.

The more she learned about Lynette, the more curious she became, and the more she wanted to know. She quickly finished her coffee and went to the kitchen for another cup. Donning a warm fleece jogging suit, she settled back comfortably on her bed and continued her reading. She felt comfort in her sanctuary and her solitude, and she could not imagine a crisis arising that would spur her into action. The snail's pace suited her today.

Chapter 11

Thursday, May 12, 1938

This afternoon is work day at the church. I could not go until Ravanell got here to be with Judge. I did not do much when I got over there, but for some reason, I was awfully tired.

Friday, May 13, 1938

Cleaned up the house today. Have not done very much this afternoon. Charles has gone for a ride tonight with Walter and Mr. Cobb in the Austin. Dr. Warrenfells came this afternoon. He says Judge's heart is in a better condition than it was Tuesday. Ravanell did not go to school today.

Cathy continued her reading through the afternoon, undisturbed. When she felt her eyelids getting heavy, she wanted to put her reading down and take a nap. However, she could not, so she went again into the bathroom and washed her face, which wakened her. Harry called around four and she reassured him that everything was fine and she could not wait to see him.

Saturday, May 14, 1938

Mable worked over at Lake Winnepesaukah today. Charles went riding with Mr. Cobb and Walter this afternoon. Baby looked better today than she did Wednesday.

Sunday, May 15, 1938

Could not go to S.S. and church today because Judge not being well. Perry came before church. Oliver and Lee came after church. Helen was here this afternoon. Mr. and Mrs. Price came awhile this afternoon. I think Judge is some better.

Mable worked over at the Lake this afternoon. Ravanell was in bed all morning, but went to Chattanooga this afternoon. *[See opposite page]*

[Sunday, May 15, 1938]

Sadie came awhile tonight. Mable is spending the night with Hattie tonight or so she says.

Monday, May 16, 1938

The orchestra is playing at the American Legion Auxiliary tonight. Mrs. Rhyne came by for Charles and Eugene Cornett.

Mable and Hattie also went. Ravanell is out somewhere with Ned. Emily and Sadie were here awhile this afternoon also Helen was here. Perry was here tonight.

Dr. Warrenfells was here this

afternoon.

Tuesday, May 17, 1938

Mrs. Hosick came over a few minutes this afternoon. I have been real busy today. I can't get out anywhere anyway. Judge is not any better.

Lake Winnepesaukah, Cathy reflected. Lake Winnie, as the locals called it, was a small amusement park built around Green Springs Lake, in Georgia, just across the Tennessee state line. The owners changed the name to Lake Winnepesaukah, which means "beautiful lake of the highlands," in Native American terms, when the swimming park opened in 1925. She and Harry used to take Michael and Heather to Lake Winnie when they were small, having no idea that Lake Winnie had been in existence in 1938.

Everyone knew about Lake Winnie and its signature ride, the Boat Chute, where couples would steal a kiss in the "tunnel of love," and so the tradition began. Even when Cathy and Harry were dating in high school, they spent a good deal of their time in the dark mill tunnel of the Boat Chute. When the kids came along, however, they were regulated to the "Kiddie Hill" section of the park.

The park had grown over the years and families would fill the picnic sheds and ride the wooden roller coaster, and the Boat Chute, cooled by the lake on muggy summer nights. A shiver went across Cathy's arm as she thought that she had traveled the same steps to the Castle and sat beneath the same southern pines as Mable had when she worked there. Cathy smiled as she wondered how many times Mable had ridden the Boat Chute.

Wednesday, May 18, 1938

Baby came as usual this morning. She looks better. Miss Mary Lizzie is quite poorly.

Thursday, May 19, 1938

The Best Speakers' Club had a picnic this afternoon after the meeting. Seab and Kerry Fox are spending the night here with Charles. Dr. Warrenfells came today. Judge is better.

Friday, May 20, 1938

The sixth grade went on a picnic to Lake Winnie today. Charles went with Mr. Cobb and Walter. He had a good time. I asked him if he had seen Mable, but he won't answer.

Saturday, May 21, 1938

Judge is still very weak. Too weak to drink cocoa.

Sunday, May 22, 1938

I did not go to S.S. and church today. Judge is not any better. Mrs. Rhyne's violin pupils gave a recital this afternoon. I asked Oliver and Lee to come sit with Judge so I could go. I thought they all did real well. It was Eugene Cornett, Barbara Anderson, Miriam Rhyne, & Charles. Frances Hammond played the piano. Baby came down for the recital.

Oliver and Lee and Mable stayed until I got back. I don't think Judge even realized I was gone. He gave me such a sweet smile when I got back. I don't think he knew that it was me.

Monday, May 23, 1938

Papa and Baby came down awhile this afternoon. They stayed with Judge so I could go to the Circle meeting. I went over to Miss Mary Lizzie's to see [C!]. He told me everything would be all right if something happened to Judge. Then we would have the money for him to leave Lucile. He'll take care of everything. I love his aroma. I can't think when I'm around him.

Dr. Warrenfells came this afternoon. He doesn't think Judge is doing very well.

Tuesday, May 24, 1938

Alders' Gate Commemoration service is being held at the church tonight. Charles has gone. He is in a play. Ravanell went out somewhere with Ned. Mable is gone with Hattie. [C!] said that he would stop by and see me. I was mighty nervous trying to get Charles off on time. I had to wait on Judge just as [C!] walked in the back door. He waited on me in the kitchen. Bless his precious heart.

After [C!] left, I gave Judge some codeine thinking it would help but he doesn't realize enough to swallow it tho I finally got him to. Gave him some more about ten o'clock and he finally got quiet.

Wednesday, May 25, 1938

I am very tired. Judge was bad all night and I slept very little. Spent most of the night between the kitchen and Judge's room. He is so weak. Too weak to eat. The cocoa has only weakened him and will not complete its task.

O, God! Give me strength. I don't know how much longer I can go on like this. Judge is going down faster now, but still he lingers. He smiled at me and told me that he really tried to love me. He did agree that what I had so often said was true, that he was too good for me. He is too sick to change his bedding but they are not badly soiled. He smiled but already there is no reaction of his pupils to the light.

As I write this later, I can say that it proved to be the last smile he gave me. His pillow pressed gently over his face ensured his final breath and sent him into the arms of Jesus. And I know that means he will never speak to me again.

Chapter 12

Cathy sat upright, rapidly reading and rereading this latest entry. The effect of the words was stunning. She collapsed on her pillows trying to fathom this latest development. *My God! She killed him! No! No! This can't be!* So she read the passage again, her heart pounding. *Yes, Lynette killed her husband in 1938!* Cathy knew that she would find no peace within herself until she could discover what had happened to Lynette.

With a shock of sudden realization, Cathy wakened to the fact that something was dreadfully wrong here, and it was up to her to make sense of it. Lynette's sin had taken her from a clandestine affair to dark scenes of murder, and had instilled a fear of being put into her proper place with a sentence of death, now that she had strayed beyond the prescribed boundaries of her station in life. Her interference with another's life path could only end in regret and dishonor. That was the way karma worked. *What goes around, comes around.* Actions sometimes come with severe consequences.

Thursday, May 26, 1938

I fell asleep on the daybed in Judge's room. Mable woke me crying that Judge was gone. I sent Ravanell to fetch Dr.

Warrenfells. Charles is very upset. Don't remember much after that except I trembled inside as Dr. Warrenfells pulled the sheet over Judge's head. Somebody called Mrs. Hosick. She came over and said that Mr. Hosick would come for the body shortly. We sat in the kitchen and I cried genuine tears. Word of Judge's passing traveled swiftly through town.

Friday, May 27, 1938

Strange to be a widow. I sat in the parlor and listened to Mable recount to numerous guests how Precious Judge had been called Home at 8:30 yesterday morning as she sat by his bed holding his hand while I slept. She told of the peaceful expression on his face as he passed and how dear he was to us all and that we only had to sit up with him for two nights.

K.C. and Lucile were here to pay their respects and I could barely look at him, yet I couldn't keep from it.

Saturday, May 28, 1938

Funeral today at 2:30. Lots of flowers and many friends called. Neighbors were all so sweet and good and thoughtful. Such a sweet funeral service by Brother Cash and Brother Story. The house seems so empty.

Sunday, May 29, 1938

I did not go to S.S. and church today. My heart is heavy as a stone. My sin is such a burden. But, I slept better tonight than I have in weeks. I can't go into Judge's room.

Monday, May 30, 1938

Went to the cemetery today. I thought I heard Judge's voice, but it was the wind I guess.

Tuesday, May 31, 1938

Don't feel like doing much today. Charles is spending the day with Kerry, and Ravanell is out somewhere with Ned. Mable is out somewhere. Went to Miss Mary Lizzie's and we prayed together all afternoon. Nothing under the milk can.

Wednesday, June 1, 1938

Aunt Ellen, Mark, Allen and Carolyn spent the night with us. They all left this morning. I did not dream that it would be this sad and lonely without Judge. His children and his grandchildren have been absolutely lovely to me.

Madge Massey took me for a ride this afternoon. We went by the cemetery again.

Thursday, June 2, 1938

How my heart aches! [C!] has not been here and I don't know where he is. I am so afraid now and I pray every day.

Mrs. Hosick came by this afternoon. Oliver and Lee and William and Helen sat till bed time with us. Maude spent the night with me last night. Kerry also stayed with Charles. He said that his father has been working in Chattanooga.

Friday, June 3, 1938

Miss Mary Lizzie came over awhile this morning. She is getting quite feeble. Charles went to the C. of C. meeting this afternoon. Helen stayed with us till bed time tonight.

Saturday, June 4, 1938

I cleaned up Judge's bedroom today. Oliver came by this afternoon. He read Judge's will.

Judge had led me to believe that I would be taken care of when he was gone. He left the house to Charles and all of his money to Mable, Sara and Ravanell. My heart is surely grieved.

Sunday, June 5, 1938

Did not go to church and S.S. today. Charles and I went up home on the twelve o'clock bus. Baby brought us back. Went to church tonight.

I'm still stunned. I don't what I'm going to do. I need to talk to [C!].

Monday, June 6, 1938

Was very busy all day today. Could not get a minute to myself. Did not go to the Missionary meeting this afternoon.

Mrs. Cash, Mrs. Peacock and also Mrs. Shaw came to see me this afternoon. They have all heard about Judge's will. Miss Annie came on the 6:30 bus.

I went to Mrs. Hosick's this morning. To Mrs. Cobb's and to Madge's for a few minutes. I cannot find [C!] anywhere. Daily Vacation Bible School began today.

Tuesday, June 7, 1938

Miss Annie and I went to see Mrs. Shaw this afternoon. Then we went over to Miss Mary Lizzie's after supper. While they talked, I checked the milk can on the back porch and found a note from [C!]. He wants to see me tomorrow. The anticipation is almost more than I can bear. I miss him so.

On our way home, I saw Hattie talking to [C!] on the corner. After I got home, Hattie came over and she and Mable went off somewhere.

I did my ironing tonight and cried.

Wednesday, June 8, 1938

Baby came as usual this morning. I

heard her sweet refrain. Miss Annie went to her aunt's with Gertrude this afternoon.

I went over to Miss Mary Lizzie's to see [C!]. She is gracious and gives us our time alone. He said that he had heard about Judge's will and told me that our plans might have to wait. I love him so much. He is precious to me.

Thursday, June 9, 1938

Maude was to come and see me today, but she called this morning and said that she was sick and could not come.

Went to the cemetery this afternoon. Wanted to be alone. It seems to lighten my heart when I can take a big cry. Charles and Kerry went to the show tonight.

Friday, June 10, 1938

Miss Annie went home on the train this afternoon. Charles and I went to the train with her.

I went over to see Emily and Tommy this afternoon. On the way home, I stopped by [C!]'s shop. When I went in, no one was around so I stepped to the back room. He was there with Hattie Winslow. He was kissing her.

My heart sank and my stomach felt sick. They did not see me and I left secretly. I went directly to the cemetery.

My anguish is more than I can bear. My heart is broken. I lay by Judge's grave and could not stop crying. Helen came by and tried to comfort me, thinking my sorrow was for Judge. Helen stayed till bed time tonight.

Chapter 13

Saturday, June 11, 1938

I tried to do my chores today, but my tears will not cease. Helen must be talking about me as I have had visitors all afternoon and still cannot stop crying. Lucile came by also. Besides Hattie, she is the last person I wanted to see right then.

Sunday, June 12, 1938

To S.S. and church today. Everyone took dinner at Lucile's today. I could not. Helen and Hattie were there. Mable said that Lucile had cooked a fine dinner. She said that today was K.C. and Lucile's wedding anniversary.

Monday, June 13, 1938

James Cash ate dinner with us. Charles went to the show tonight. I started teaching Betty Allen this morning.

Tuesday, June 14, 1938

Walter Cobb spent the night with Charles. They went to the show. Helen came and stayed until bed time.

Mable has gone somewhere with Hattie (?)

Wednesday, June 15, 1938

Went to see Dr. Warrenfells. He will not give me a shot for my headache. My shock is overwhelming. He tells me that I am going to have a baby. O, God, help me this dark day! The baby is due around February 27. I am so sick.

Thursday, June 16, 1938

Went to church tonight. Daily Bible School closed with exercises .The Rev. Fritts was the song leader. Charles goes to the swimming pool nearly every day now. I need to talk to [C!]. I need him so much.

Friday, June 17, 1938

I told Mable, Ravanell and Charles about the baby. Their shock was almost as great as mine. I'll tell Baby tomorrow.

No one says anything. They just look at me. Charles is so precious. We went to church tonight.

Saturday, June 18, 1938

Baby is such a precious sister. When I told her my news, she told me not to worry and that everything would be all right. Charles wanted to go home with Baby this morning, but his daddy is picking him up this afternoon. I guess he heard that Judge left him the house. Hattie and Helen spent the night with Mable. Lucile came over awhile tonight. I went to church. I didn't want to be in the house with them.

Sunday, June 19, 1938

Hattie stayed until after dinner and then she and Helen left and went home. I went to church but Mable and Ravanell did not go. Slept awhile after dinner and then Tom and Maude and Baby came awhile. Baby asked me to move back up home with them. I told her I could not, so she told me to come with them and she would bring me back which she did. A big rain came just about time for church but I went anyway.

Monday, June 20, 1938

Went to church this morning. I pray more than ever these days. Mable and I decided that she would pay $5 a week as her and Ravanell's part of the expenses here.

To Miss Mary Lizzie's this afternoon. She said that my cards were not favorable and that they reveal my sin, but she is the keeper of my secrets.

Tuesday, June 21, 1938

To church today. No word from [C!]. Mable did not come home for dinner.

I am resting more these days than I have for a number of years. But soon I'll have to get to work at something. To Dr. Warrenfells this afternoon for some headache powder. To church tonight. Brother Cash preached a fine sermon on Christ.

Am alone again tonight. Ravanell came in early but left again with Ned. I wonder what [C!] is doing. Mable and Hattie are out in Chattanooga somewhere.

Wednesday, June 22, 1938

To church today. Baby stayed for church. I wanted her to stay all day but she said Papa was not feeling well and that she better get back. I did the washing this afternoon and then to Miss Mary Lizzie's. I found a note under the milk can. I'll see him tomorrow.

CHAPTER 14

Thursday, June 23, 1938

O! The darkest day of my life! There is no end to my sin. I met [C!] at Miss Mary Lizzie's. She is not feeling well and rested and slept all afternoon.

[C!] and I met in the garden shed and I tried to tell him about the baby but he had already heard. He said things have changed and I did not understand. He said that we needed to stay away from each other for awhile and I asked him if it was because of Judge or Hattie. The color drained from his face in an instant and he said we could no longer go on. I felt sick inside and fell at his feet begging him not to go. He said that even though he loved me he could not be with me. [See opposite page] [Thursday June 23, 1938].

I do know how it happened. He turned to walk away and I jumped up and held him and he pushed me away. He shook his head and turned his back to me and somehow the shovel found its way into

> *my hands and then came crashing down on the back of his head. I didn't mean to do it, it just happened and my beloved lay dead at my feet. I cannot fathom this. I must call Baby. O, K.C. Fox! Why did you do this to me!*

Cathy's head was reeling. *She's killed her husband! She's killed her lover! Who is this woman?* She tried to remember if she had heard any stories about murder and mayhem in a small Georgia town in the thirties, but no such recollections came to mind.

She spent the next few minutes rereading this passage to make sure in her mind that she was not mistaken. It had been inconceivable to her that Lynette would meet K.C. for their tryst in any mood other than romance, let alone death. Cathy could only imagine Lynette breathing so hard that her body rose and fell as though crossing an invisible washboard, shaking him in mortal terror at what she had done, pleading with him to live, only to find his head lolling lifeless on his shoulders.

Her first encounter of humanity against humanity in hatred left her nauseated at the sound, much like the cracking of an egg, which had left her lover's lifeless eyes staring up at her, not knowing why. He did not awaken with wicked laughter at having almost frightened her to death, and felt no amorous embrace. She slumped over him and pressing her velvet lips to his, she found that his kiss was as dead as he was, and she threw herself upon his corpse, sobbing her heart out. Cathy could only imagine Lynette's panic, and now felt wide awake and pressed forward.

Friday, June 24, 1938

In the darkest hours of the morning, I called Baby and she came to my rescue. I took her to Miss Mary Lizzie's garden shed and together we put [C!] in the back of her milk truck and took him up home. Papa was asleep and never knew she was gone. In the barn, Baby started singing, "Died in the millpond, died in the millpond, died in the millpond..." and I knew what we must do. His dismemberment was more than I could take and I threw up profusely. Baby's strength and fortitude completed the deed. [See opposite page] [Friday, June 24, 1938]

She packed his body into four milk cans and we transported him in her milk truck to the millpond. Shielded by darkness, she had punched holes in the tops of the cans and we rowed silently out into the millpond & lowered my lover to his watery tomb. I shall never forget the sound of the milk cans sinking. Baby went back up home before daybreak and I'm still crying. To church today to pray and pray and pray.

Saturday, June 25, 1938

I went to the cemetery and cried. Across the meadow I could see the millpond and my heart ached.

Went to Miss Mary Lizzie's this afternoon. She knows something is wrong, but we don't speak of it. I have not heard from Charles in Nashville. Went to church tonight and prayed.

Sunday, June 26, 1938

To Sunday School and church today. Lucile is beside herself as K.C. did not come home. They are searching for him.

Ravanell and Ned went away somewhere today and Mable to the Lake. I am alone and I am glad of it. A big rain came this afternoon and I sat alone in the darkness and contemplated my sin.

Monday, June 27, 1938

Baby came this morning and I heard her singing "Go Tell Aunt Rhody" as she came up the back steps. She was very kind to me and we did not speak of [C!]. She wants me to move up home. Went to the Mission Study class this afternoon.

Tuesday, June 28, 1938

To the Mission Study class again this afternoon. Mrs. Ruth Lee is the speaker. She came and stayed awhile today and I wanted her to go home. She finally did.

Mable is out with Hattie somewhere. Ravanell is gone with Ned.

Wednesday, June 29, 1938

Went to the Mission Study class again. Mrs. Ruth Lee said that they are still searching for K.C. Lucile cried during class. I went home alone today and went to prayer meeting tonight.

Thursday, June 30, 1938

I don't know how much longer I can go on like this. The Devil has stolen my soul! I try to put all these misdeeds out of my mind.

Made blackberry jam and jelly for when Charles gets back from Nashville. To the Mission Study class this afternoon.

To the cemetery. To Miss Mary Lizzie's.

Friday, July 1, 1938

I am sick these days. My headaches are frequent. I don't know if I can carry this baby. I don't know if I can live.

Mable and Ravanell are both out somewhere and I am alone in the darkness. O, God! Please bring relief to my tortured soul!

Saturday, July 2, 1938

Talk in town now is that K.C. is either off dead somewhere or has run off and left Lucile and the children. The Sheriff is still searching. Went to the cemetery and cried at Judge's grave as I gazed at the millpond. Neighbors think I mourn Judge. My heart is turning to stone. I hate [C!] for what he has brought me to.

Sunday, July 3, 1938

Charles came home this morning on the bus. I was not looking for him until in the morning. To Miss Mary Lizzie's for a few minutes this morning. She is so very kind to me.

Studied my S.S. lesson this afternoon. Charles went to the Lake to see Mable. We have heard that Mrs. Cash has been called to her Heavenly Home.

Monday, July 4, 1938

Helped Ravanell fix her picnic lunch this morning. She and Ned and Ruth and Clarence have gone off somewhere for the day.

Mable did not come home. Charles said that she had met a man at the Lake and was talking to him when he left. We are alone this afternoon until he went over to Kerry Fox's. Baby came tonight and took us all to the Lake for fireworks. Independence Day.

Tuesday, July 5, 1938

Miss Mary Lizzie is much worse. I

stayed with her quite a while this afternoon. Dr. Warrenfells says that as sick as she is, she won't last much longer. She is 93.

Wednesday, July 6, 1938

Hudson Chambers stopped by this afternoon. He informed me that the house is going to be sold and he is going to take Charles back to Nashville to live with him. I have raised Charles since his mama died when he was five and I don't know how I can part with him. If Judge were still alive, Hud wouldn't want him. I don't think Charles knows yet of this decision. I need to tell the girls.

Thursday, July 7, 1938

Gathered Charles, Mable and Ravanell at breakfast to talk to them. Charles said that he had liked Nashville. Mable and Ravanell did protest about moving but no one said much.

Went over to Miss Mary Lizzie's this afternoon. She is some better but still is very sick. She wants me to move into her house when Judge's house is sold.

Friday, July 8, 1938

My beloved has been gone two weeks. And I can do nothing to bring him back. To turn back the clock would be a blessing and a comfort that can never be.

Oliver took me to Mr. State's office to check on Judge's insurance. Once again he is not my beloved benefactor. The monies are to be divided equally among Sara, Mable, Ravanell and Charles. Oliver sensed my disappointment. Damn you, Judge for your deceit!

Saturday, July 9, 1938

Went back over to Miss Mary Lizzie's and spent the night with her. Her condition is severely weakened and Dr. Warrenfells has sent a practical nurse.

Sunday, July 10, 1938

Did not go to S.S. and church today. Stayed with Miss Mary Lizzie. Papa and Baby came down today and Louise stayed with Miss Mary Lizzie while I visited them.

Don't know where Mable and Ravanell have gone. Charles and Walter Cobb have gone swimming this afternoon.

CHAPTER 15

Monday, July 11, 1938

I have moved most of my things over to Miss Mary Lizzie's. Have not told Charles, Mable or Ravanell. Louise comes every day to take care of Miss Mary Lizzie. She is so feeble now.

Tuesday, July 12, 1938

Washed today. Did not get the clothes dry before a big rain came this afternoon. Charles has gone to a melon cutting at the parsonage this afternoon.

Wednesday, July 13, 1938

Did my ironing this afternoon. Oliver came this afternoon and brought the checks to Mable, Ravanell and Charles. He sent Sara's to her in Chattanooga.

Did not sleep well tonight. Went to bed early.

Thursday, July 14, 1938

Ravanell plans to go to college in

September. There's still hope for her. The girls went over to Hattie's and went for a ride in her car and had tire trouble.

Friday, July 15, 1938

Aunt Ellen came down with Baby this morning and stayed while she delivered milk. The girls played tennis this morning and then went to the swimming pool. Mable stays gone a lot now. She and Hattie seem to always have someone to see or some place to go.

Saturday, July 16, 1938

I took care of Miss Mary Lizzie all day. Did not get to sit down till about four o'clock. But I am not very tired. Charles left for Nashville with Hud today. It was almost more than I could bear. I'm still crying.

Louise stayed with Miss Mary Lizzie tonight while I went to prayer meeting at the Baptist church. Mr. Story made a good talk. The girls are gone out somewhere.

Sunday, July 17, 1938

To S.S. and church. Did not fix a big Sunday dinner. Just a little dinner for Miss Mary Lizzie, Louise and me. Lucile brought over some tomatoes from her garden. I'll can them tomorrow. My heart aches for Charles.

Monday, July 18, 1938

Oliver came by this afternoon. He is angry that Hud is selling the house. He said that he told Hud that Judge left the house to Charles so that he would have a home. Hud said that he did have a home in Nashville. Mr. Hosick is buying the house if they can get together on a price to make the trade.

Mable and Hattie have moved into a rooming house near the Lake, or so Helen told us this afternoon.

Tuesday, July 19, 1938

This has been an awfully rainy day. Mable is at the Lake and Ravanell and Ned are out somewhere.

Emily said that Tommy and some of the others are still searching for K.C. Fox. She said they are searching the woods over in Pea Vine today.

Wednesday, July 20, 1938

Mrs. Hosick came over to visit Miss Mary Lizzie today. Several neighbors have stopped by. Louise is here. And so am I.

It has been a very busy day. Sometimes I barely have time to sit down. I miss Charles. I miss his precious smile.

Thursday, July 21, 1938

Received a letter from Charles. He is having a good time with Hud and his new wife in Nashville.

I made some sheets for Madge this afternoon. Every little bit helps. I am so sick to my stomach.

Friday, July 22, 1938

The sickness is still with me and I can imagine the wagging tongues. Miss Mary Lizzie tells me not to worry. I busy myself with chores but have to lie down with a damp cloth to ease my headaches.

Saturday, July 23, 1938

Mrs. Hosick and I went up to see Mrs. Shaw, Mrs. Hammond and Mrs. Peacock today. We went to the Baptist Church to the prayer meeting tonight.

Hud brought Charles home today to get the rest of his things. What has become of my family? Mable is gone, I don't know where Ravanell is and now Hud has taken my beloved Charles away from me. It is all slipping away. [C!] has been gone a month. I need to see Dr. Warrenfells.

Cathy thought back to the night that she had extricated the diary from its hiding place, and felt very perplexed at the discoveries that she had made. The weight of these discoveries lay heavy on her heart, for she knew that she would not be able to tell anyone about them. The gravity of the ramifications could alter so many lives that the karmic effect seemed horribly insurmountable to her. The passage about the death of Georgia Turner's baby had intrigued her, and she hadn't even reached that part yet. It made her wonder if other surprises were in store.

The diary would be finished tonight, she made up her mind, for there was no telling what else she would find. Whatever the outcome, Cathy's burning desire to know stood at the forefront. She would see it through to the end, and once and for all, shatter the written confession and free it from the musty pages. Once finished, the legwork would begin and she decided that she would enlist Gigi's aid to complete it.

Before continuing her reading, Cathy took her place at her computer, surfing web sites, searching superficially, for any news stories or information about disappearance, murder, or assault in Walker County in the thirties. Nothing came to light and she expanded and narrowed her searches repeatedly. Frustrated, she made her way to the kitchen where she popped some popcorn and retrieved a soda and another pack of cigarettes.

Her frustration gave way to discontent as she settled back on her pillows to read the diary in its entirety. *Had Judge and K.C. Fox reached out through time and space and the Cosmos to contact her? And, if so, why?*

Or, did Lynette, whether consciously or not, want to be caught and punished for her crimes? And, why was Cathy chosen for this assignment? She felt that she was not special, but had been contacted by special people.

Chapter 16

Sunday, July 24, 1938

Went to S.S. and church this morning. When I got back to Judge's house, I found a note from Ravanell on the kitchen table. She has run off to Florida with Ned. O, Ravanell, what are you doing? This house is so empty. My family is gone. My life is over. There is no point to it.

Monday, July 25, 1938

Went up home this afternoon on the twelve o'clock bus. Was sick all the way. It was an hour late. Baby brought me back to Miss Mary Lizzie's. It rained awfully hard on us before we got here.

Tuesday, July 26, 1938

Mrs. Myers and Virginia and their cousin, Miss Nash, came awhile to see Miss Mary Lizzie. She seemed glad to see them.

Ellen, Madge and I went to prayer meeting at the Baptist church tonight. I pray for Charles and wonder how he is getting along. I pray for Mable and Ravanell. I pray for myself. God, forgive me.

Wednesday, July 27, 1938

Hattie and Mable stopped by today. Mable moved the furniture out of the house. Little by little our home has lost its life and will soon be gone. Hattie said that Mable had broken up with her boy friend. It's just as well. She never introduced him.

Aunt Ellen came down with Baby today on the milk truck. She will stay with Miss Mary Lizzie and me until Baby's next run.

Thursday, July 28, 1938

Georgia Turner's baby died last night. The crib death. When she woke up it was gone. O, the sorrow in her home today. She is inconsolable.

Friday, July 29, 1938

Aunt Ellen went back up home with Baby today. I baked my cakes for Sunday and took one over to Georgia Turner's house. She is not doing well at all.

Louise stayed with Miss Mary Lizzie.

Saturday, July 30, 1938

It was such a lovely little funeral. Such a sweet angel. She wore a dress that her grandma had made for her. A little white lace dress.

Georgia's heartache is unbearable. I cried for her tonight and I cried for me.

Sunday, July 31, 1938

Went to S.S. and church. Such a sad day! Lucile told me that Georgia Turner had hanged herself in the garage. Her note said that she could not go on knowing that her baby was in the cold ground. Edsel is beside himself. His loss is overwhelming.

Monday, August 1, 1938

I stayed with Miss Mary Lizzie while Louise went over to Hosick's to see Georgia Turner. Then she stayed while I went. Nothing but death and dying these days. Mr. Hosick completed his trade with Hud. Our home is gone.

Tuesday, August 2, 1938

As we stood around Georgia's grave I looked over to Judge's grave and then over the meadow to the millpond. I felt a fluttering in my middle & sick all of a sudden.

I wonder where Georgia is right now. However, it was a lovely graveside service and Georgia was laid to rest.

Wednesday, August 3, 1938

I yearn for Charles so much. I even miss Ravanell and Mable. Miss Mary Lizzie is still weak and I sit with her each day and sometimes hold her hand.

Baby came as usual but did not stay long.

Thursday, August 4, 1938

Miss Mary Lizzie's 94th birthday. Cordia and Emily brought a group from the Presbyterian church to see her and Brother Cash brought a group from the Baptist church.

Miss Mary Lizzie is still lucid and was glad to see everyone. She is most beloved in this community.

Friday, August 5, 1938

I baked my meatloaf for Sunday dinner and baked some cakes. I read the cards for Miss Mary Lizzie, but did not tell her what they truly revealed.

Saturday, August 6, 1938

A red bird alighted on the window sill of Miss Mary Lizzie's room and pecked four times. Four days, four weeks, four months, or four years. In my heart of hearts I knew it meant weeks and I knew that Miss Mary Lizzie would soon be gone.

Sunday, August 7, 1938

Homecoming day at Rock Spring today. Sara and Madge took me and Baby brought me back. We stayed with Papa a couple of hours.

Went to the Baptist Church tonight for prayer. The slight movements in my stomach bring me comfort and dread. I cannot explain it. No one would understand.

Monday, August 8, 1938

Went to the W.M.S. meeting this afternoon. Mable and Hattie were there. The Frigidaire is not doing well and K.C. Fox is not here to fix it. Maybe Mr. Richard can do it. He has bought the shop from Lucile.

I don't hear from Charles these days. Nor Ravanell.

Tuesday, August 9, 1938

Tom and Maude came down and spent the day with Miss Mary Lizzie and me. Baby brought them but she had to get back and came and collected them this evening. Baby is so dear to me. And so is Maude. I enjoyed seeing them so very much.

Wednesday, August 10, 1938

Baby told me that Emily has a nine pound baby boy that came about six o'clock this morning. I can imagine how proud Tommy is. I can see him handing out cigars at the barber shop. No prayer meeting at either of the churches or on this side of town tonight. Louise left early today and I stayed and sat with Miss Mary Lizzie while she slept. My future is so uncertain. I guess when Miss Mary Lizzie is called Home, I'll move to Rock Spring with Baby and Papa.

Thursday, August 11, 1938

Have been quite busy today. Rested tonight when I got through ironing. My sleep is so fitful.

Friday, August 12, 1938

I had a dream about [C!] but I cannot remember all of it. I think about him all of the time. Baby and I have never spoken of him since that fateful night. Have worked quite a bit today.

Saturday, August 13, 1938

Papa came down with Baby this morning. He gets around quite well for his age. Have not read and studied much today. Lucile took her children to visit her sister in Cloudland.

Lord, help me as I stumble.

Sunday, August 14, 1938

To S.S. and church this morning. Louise stayed with Miss Mary Lizzie. When I got home Ravanell and Ned were here. They had gotten married in Macon on the way to Florida. She said that she and Ned have settled in a little town called Steinhatchie and Ned works at a gas station there. They went over to stay with Mable tonight.

Monday, August 15, 1938

Went to the Circle meeting at Emily's this afternoon. She told me that Mrs. Potts was going back to Florida with Ravanell and Ned at the end of the week. I don't know how that's going to work out. Ned and Emily's mother is not the easiest person in the world to get along with. How she can leave that precious baby, I don't know.

Tuesday, August 16, 1938

Miss Mary Lizzie is a wonderful woman. She is so devoted and is such an inspiration to everyone. Mrs. Shaw and Mrs. Center came to see her today.

Wednesday, August 17, 1938

Louise went to her aunt's place this afternoon. She will be back in a few days. Mr. Jamie McAuliffe is a corpse at the Hosick Funeral Home. He succumbed to a fever. I went over there awhile for a few minutes to see Madge while Miss Mary Lizzie slept.

Thursday, August 18, 1938

Wash day.

Friday, August 19, 1938

I could not go to Jamie McAuliffe's funeral because I could not leave Miss Mary Lizzie alone. I busied myself all day with the ironing and housework.

Chapter 17

Saturday, August 20, 1938

Ravanell and Ned and Mrs. Potts have gone back to Florida. Louise came back today and stayed with Miss Mary Lizzie so I could go up home to see Papa.

Sunday, August 21, 1938

Tom and Maude left for Huntsville to bring Mrs. Shields for a visit. They left about seven o'clock this morning.

I stayed in LaFayette with Mrs. Hammond this morning to S.S. and church. I guess the widows seem to find each other. Miss Annie was there.

Sara took me up home after church and I helped Baby get the milking done. She brought me back.

Monday, August 22, 1938

Miss Mary Lizzie and I had a blessed Prayer time together this morning as we have had several days since I have been here.

Louise stayed this afternoon so I could go over and see Emily and the baby. The dog days of summer are so insufferable. I'm stuck on the wheel of life.

Tuesday, August 23, 1938

I am so sick today but the washing and ironing has to be done. I let out some of my dresses this afternoon. [C!] has been gone two months today.

Wednesday, August 24, 1938

Washed some more today but let those things wait until tomorrow to iron.

Thursday, August 25, 1938

Oliver came this afternoon to see Miss Mary Lizzie and I ironed in the kitchen while they talked business.

Louise went on a picnic today with her boyfriend at the Municipal park. Mable and Hattie went with them.

* * *

Friday, August 26, 1938

After I finished the house, Louise stayed with Miss Mary Lizzie so that I could go to the cemetery. The evening is hot and I don't feel so well.

I wish things could have been different. I wish I had never met Judge or K.C. Fox. My life is ruined beyond repair. I feel better tho after my cry.

Saturday, August 27, 1938

Went to help Emily with her baby, Joe, this afternoon. He cries lots. She's not feeling very well. Maude and Tom got back to Chattanooga with Mrs. Shields.

Sunday, August 28, 1938

To S.S. and church today. Did not fix a Sunday dinner. Madge sat with Miss Mary Lizzie while I took the four o'clock train to Chattanooga to see Maude and Tom. While I was waiting on the bus on Market Street, Tom and Maude came by and picked me up. What a blessing!

Monday, August 29, 1938

I enjoyed my visit with Maude and Tom. They brought me back to L—late last night. The mail brings no news of Charles. I miss that precious boy so much. I wonder if he has started school. I'm sure he is very busy. Hud does not see fit to let me know how the little fellow is doing.

Tuesday, August 30, 1938

Made a shirt for Charles today. I don't know why. Mable and Hattie came by and ate dinner with Miss Mary Lizzie and me. Mable looks like she has a black eye and tries to cover it with makeup. But no. there was no mention how she got it.

Wednesday, August 31, 1938

I let some more of my dresses out. They are getting tight and I'm trying not to show. Miss Mary Lizzie is so kind to me. She understands me so well.

To Prayer meeting tonight.

Thursday, September 1, 1938

I have been anxious and nervous all day. I can't help but think of the red bird. It has been about three weeks.

Friday, September 2, 1938

Worked hard all day cleaning the house and the closets. Studied my S.S. lesson tonight for a long time. Just before nine, Miss Mary Lizzie handed me her cards and as I sat holding her hand she lapsed into unconsciousness. I called Dr. Warrenfells.

Saturday, September 3, 1938

Miss Mary Lizzie has not awakened. I took it easy today and really did nothing.

Sunday, September 4, 1938

Louise came and sat with Miss Mary Lizzie while I went to S.S. and church. She is still not awake. I fixed us some dinner and then sat by Miss Mary Lizzie's bed and read my Bible.

My soul is hollow now. The weight of my sins crushes me. Perhaps one day I'll go to sleep and not awaken. It would feel so much better than the way I feel now. I have destroyed so many people. I have destroyed myself. I have destroyed my soul.

CHAPTER 18

Monday, September 5, 1938

Miss Mary Lizzie has been unconscious since Friday. I am so saddened for I know it will not be long now. I called Baby and told her. Miss Annie and Mrs. Bender came to see Miss Mary Lizzie but they did not stay long. That in brackets on the opposite page should be on this page.

Tuesday, September 6, 1938

[Louise was needed at Emily's so I stayed with Miss Mary Lizzie].

Dr. Warrenfells stopped by and said he was going to check on Emily and would send Louise back. He left about 12:30.

I was so tired and had lain down for awhile. Miss Mary Lizzie was resting comfortably. About 2:15 I woke up suddenly. When I looked at the ceiling it looked like coals of fire were falling down on top of me. The fright was so bad that when I sat up I felt so sick and all I could do was to hold my stomach. When I gathered my wits, I could see no coals of fire, just the darkened room. Then it occurred to me to check on Miss Mary Lizzie.

Her countenance was so serene and I knew that Jesus had called her Home. Never more would her lips speak to me; I wanted so to hear her voice. My sorrow is deep. My tears are genuine. Four weeks.

Wednesday, September 7, 1938

I went to Hosick's to see Miss Mary Lizzie about 11:00. Lots of pretty flowers. Mrs. Hosick said that Miss Mary Lizzie's funeral was set for this afternoon at two o'clock. When I asked her why so soon, she said that Miss Mary Lizzie wanted it that way.

Thursday, September 8, 1938

There is no more life in this house today. An agent came to the door inquiring about the purchase of Miss Mary Lizzie's property. Miss Mary Lizzie is not yet cold in her grave and the vultures appear. Went to the cemetery. The flowers on her grave are beautiful. My baby moves frequently and I've decided if it's a girl, I am going to name her Mary Elizabeth.

Friday, September 9, 1938

I did not feel like doing the washing and ironing this afternoon but I did it anyway. Miss Mary Lizzie's room is so empty and I can almost see her lying in bed.

Saturday, September 10, 1938

Have not felt well today but kept going anyway. Received a letter from Charles. He has started school in Nashville. He is in the seventh grade and he says he likes it. No word from Mable or Ravanell.

Sunday, September 11, 1938

Emily brought the baby over for a little while and said that when my time comes she has some things she can give me. I told her that I was probably going to move to Rock Spring with Papa and Baby.

She told me that Lucile had lost the house last week and she and her children were living permanently with her sister in Cloudland.

O, [C!]! What havoc you have wreaked on so many of us! Look what you have done!

Monday, September 12, 1938

Baby came to see me this morning.

She is such a comfort. Oliver stopped by and told me not to be in a hurry to pack my things. He said that we would be discussing that later. Baby and I were puzzled.

Tuesday, September 13, 1938

Lake Winnepesaukah closed Sunday night so Mable is not working there anymore.

She and Hattie drove to Marietta today to take a Civil Service examination.

Wednesday, September 14, 1938

Went up to Mrs. Jennings's a few minutes to see about a bed I loaned her last year. I told Emily that if Mrs. Jennings did not want to buy it, she could have it. However, it turned out that Mrs. Jennings said she wanted to keep it and paid me two dollars.

Went by the cemetery on the way home. Eva Smith saw me and stopped and asked me to ride to Prayer meeting with her tonight.

Thursday, September 15, 1938

Have tried so hard to have a quiet time to study and pray but those times come seldom now. Mable and Hattie have moved to Chattanooga.

The orchestra is to play at the American Legion Auxiliary this afternoon. I had planned to go but don't think I could bear to hear them without Charles. I am alone tonight. I think of Miss Mary Lizzie.

Friday, September 16, 1938

I have felt unusually well today. Did the house cleaning and baked a cake. And other things and I am not so very tired. Tho my back hurts some.

Did not want to fix dinner just for myself, but Oliver Graham called just before noon and said that he would stop by to talk some business. I guess Miss Mary Lizzie's house has been sold.

I fixed our dinner and after dinner he read Miss Mary Lizzie's will. What a sweet dear loving benefactor! She wanted me and my child to have a home and has left me her house, so now I do not have to move! She also left some monies to pay the taxes. What a glorious day! I started crying and could not stop. Oliver was very patient with me and told me he would take care of the legals.

I rested for the first time in a long long time after he left.

Chapter 19

Saturday, September 17, 1938

Baby came as usual and I fixed our breakfast and told her my unexpected good fortune. She was joyous and was singing when she left. Just the ordinary routine today except I'm in my own home where I cannot be removed. I have told no one about this. I fell to my knees and cried and gave thanks to my Almighty God for orchestrating my deliverance.

Sunday, September 18, 1938

To S.S .and church. I could tell by the hushed whispers that the Sisterhood has heard of my good fortune.

Sara took me up home after church and Baby brought me back. I noticed my dresses are tighter and I can't let them out anymore.

Monday, September 19, 1938

I went to town this afternoon to look at washing machines. Just in case mine goes down and I need a new one. Emily brought some baby things by the house. She also brought me some clothes. My baby moves daily and I'm not so sick. I did a big washing today and did the ironing tonight.

Baby was here this afternoon. I read the cards for her but I do not charge her. She is so dear to me. Emily came by later for her reading and wanted to pay me the fifty cents, but I told her that I could not accept it. She has been so good to me.

Tuesday, September 20, 1938

I walked to the cemetery this morning. It was chilly. I miss dear sweet Miss Mary Lizzie. I could not help but to gaze at the millpond. My shame and my blight. The Sheriff still looks for K.C. Fox. I studied and prayed tonight.

Cathy reflected on the recent turn of events with the awareness that Lynette had actually experienced the emotional upheaval, and had lived through it. *What does she do now? How does she manage?*

Week by week had passed until the final flicker of Judge's life had dropped into mere conversation; into occasional mention, and then into silence. And, week by week, the lines of maternity had deepened in Lynette's face until she was all mother, yet still childless.

In spite of the saving grace of a baby, gossip and opinions passed back and forth throughout the Church and the Sisterhood. Though she was not untidy, or coarse in mind or body, she was eyed suspiciously by those considered to be the most Christian, not that they thought her to be an inveterate sinner, but rather, somehow, just slightly dishonest. They just didn't know how.

Of all the bitterness of the world, not being necessary would be the most bitter, Cathy reasoned. With a deep, simple nature, a nature of brooding love, Lynette Stinson had nothing in her life but the crumbs that fell from richer tables: her neighbors' friendly acceptance of those services she was grateful to provide.

Despite her reactionary role in Life, self-preservation had guided her, and Destiny placed her where she needed to be. She remained faithful to God, proffering oblation for her shortcomings, even though all she had ever really wanted was something to call her own.

* * *

Lynette crossed the hallway and opened Judge's bedroom door and was instantly met with a blast of icy air that almost tore the door from its hinges. The noise was terrific, as though a storm had leaped into the room, raging and terrifying. She moved swiftly into the room and wanted to slam the door, to cry for help, to find someone.

Suddenly, she saw Judge, and the terror was upon her. She did not want to speak to him. The heavy brocaded bedspread had been blown back and she could see where he had lain and had taken his last breath. The air was sharp and took on the acrid smell of fallen oak leaves, almost taking her breath away. Judge raised his right arm and opened his mouth to speak, but all Lynette could see was the gaping hole in his face, and the look of hatred in his eyes that struck terror in her heart. Then, suddenly, she was looking into the eyes of K.C. Fox, whose skull was split and drenched in his own blood.

* * *

Cathy awoke with a start, not knowing how long she had slept. Darkness had gathered in her room and she fumbled for the switch on the lamp while she stared at the flashing blue circular light on her computer. *Ten fifteen. Did I sleep that long?* She tried to recall the day, but could not; only that she had read and slept. She jumped up and went to the kitchen to fix a sandwich and grab a soda. She desperately wanted to finish the diary tonight. Harry called and their conversation was brief, as he would be home soon.

Wednesday, September 21, 1938

Have not accomplished anything today.

Thursday, September 22, 1938

Have not felt well today. Did just as little as I could get by with. Mable came from Chattanooga to see me. She said she and Hattie are working in Chattanooga now.

She suggested that if I am going to remain in this house that I might want to take in a boarder so I will not be alone when my time comes. I don't know if her concern was genuine or if she was hinting for a place to stay. Surely she has not spent all of Judge's money. I told her that I would consider it.

Friday, September 23, 1938

Lucile and her children came by to see

me today. Hope my nervous and upset did not show. They came to move the last of their things to her sister's in Cloudland. The visit was not long; it just seemed that way. [C!] has been gone three months today.

Saturday, September 24, 1938

Baby came by as usual today and I told her about Mable's suggestion and Baby agreed. She said that it would be a good idea to have someone in the house to fetch Dr. Warrenfells when my time comes. I'll start looking for someone next week.

Sunday, September 25, 1938

To S.S. and church. Did not go up home after church today. Eva Smith picked me up and we went to the Baptist church tonight. Revival services began there today.

Monday, September 26, 1938

Mrs. Graham called and said she was sending a woman over to see about boarding with me. How news does travel in this town! I cleaned up the West room upstairs.

Miss Myrtle Henderson from the Grammar school arrived this afternoon and we struck our bargain that she would board in the West room and pay *me $5 per week. I hope she works out. She is older, but nice.*

I did not go to church tonight.

Tuesday, September 27, 1938

I went to the bank and deposited the $5 from Miss Myrtle and the $2.50 that I made from reading cards last week. I cannot touch the tax monies from Miss Mary Lizzie because that will insure me a home.

My bank account is better now and every little bit helps. I am hoping to get another boarder. I need to make deposits while I can. I have to think of my sweet little Mary Elizabeth.

Wednesday, September 28, 1938

I have heard nothing of Charles. I hope he is all right. How I miss that dear sweet boy. O, to go back to the time when he and Kerry played on the front porch and the girls came and went and Judge needed me. But I know that can be no more.

Life has changed so much and I take the changes as gracefully as possible. Being Judge's widow helps. Baby came as usual.

Thursday, September 29, 1938

Mable came to see me again. She says that Hattie is moving back home with Dr.

and Mrs. Winslow. She did not say what has happened in Chattanooga. But she did say that she would feel much better if she stayed with me and know that I would not be alone in my time of need. She must be in need of money but she still drives Judge's automobile tho.

I agreed for her to stay in the East room, then we went upstairs and moved some things out of the room so she could move in. Maybe later she will tell me what has transpired.

Friday, September 30, 1938

Mable moved her things in today and I fixed dinner for her, Miss Henderson and myself.

Went up home on the twelve o'clock bus and Baby brought me back. I baked a cake tonight for Mrs. Loughridge. She owes me for two cakes now.

Saturday, October 1, 1938

Mable drove me over to see Mrs. Loughridge. Took the cake over there and she paid me for both of them.

Mable went to town to help with the election today. Miss Henderson went to Chattanooga today. Went to see Emily this afternoon but she was not at home.

I was disappointed this afternoon for I had planned—

I baked a cake using the yolks I had

left over from last night. I did not sleep well.

Sunday, October 2, 1938

To S.S. and church. Did not go up home this afternoon.

Mable and Hattie went for a ride out somewhere.

Monday, October 3, 1938

Mable went to work at the courthouse this morning. I guess being Judge's daughter still helps her.

Baby came for a few minutes this morning. She said that Helen had married William Derryberry on Saturday. They have been sparking for some time now.

Emily spent the day with us and I went with her to see Dr. Warrenfells. He circumcised Little Joe today. Miss Annie was at Emily's this evening to help.

Tuesday, October 4, 1938

I went to the bank this morning and made my deposit. I washed and ironed this afternoon and did not finish till late. I did not go to church tonight. Everyone else went. Decided I'd rather read and pray since I'd be alone.

I pray fervently for Charles. He is such a precious boy and I love him dearly. The emptiness in my life since he left is almost overwhelming. I miss him so. I hope he will not be a rough boy as he grows up. I hope the big city does not change him.

Chapter 20

Wednesday, October 5, 1938

Baby came as usual this morning. She wants me to go up and stay with Papa while she goes to the W.M.S. meeting at Kensington. I went to church this morning to some kind of district meeting. Only a few were there. Went to the cemetery this afternoon. I still cry but not as much. My sorrow is deep. I cannot get over how blue the sky is and how beautiful the leaves are turning this autumn. Went to prayer meeting tonight.

Thursday, October 6, 1938

Mrs. Hosick paid me to wash four blankets for her this morning. I'm doing washing while I still can but it gets harder and harder with the passing days.

Went on the twelve o'clock bus up home this afternoon to stay with Papa while Baby went to the W.M.S. meeting at Kensington. Baby brought me home. Only Miss Myrtle and me here tonight.

Friday, October 7, 1938

I received a letter from Hudson Chambers today. He is having difficulty with Charles. He said that Charles broke his arm at school last week. It makes me wonder.

Mable worked at the courthouse and Miss Myrtle went on a bird watching picnic this afternoon with the Audubon Society in Chattanooga.

Saturday, October 8, 1938

After dinner today, I went over to Emily's for a little while. She has a cold this week. Little Joe is getting along all right.

When I arrived back home, lo and behold, the sight and the blessing! Charles saw me and flew from the porch to my arms. His few belongings were in bundles on the porch and he said that his daddy had dropped him off for a visit and would return for him.

I told Charles to put his things in the back room and then I brought him to the kitchen for some chocolate cake and milk while I fixed a sling for his precious little broken arm. While he was eating, I looked in his belongings and found a letter from Hud to me. He said that if I loved Charles so much that I could have him. I don't know how to tell Charles that his [See opposite page] Saturday October 8, 1938 daddy is not coming back for him. Hudson did not return and I put Charles to bed tonight. I wrote a letter to Hud and asked him to send the remainder of Charles's money, but I don't expect that I will receive an answer.

Sunday, October 9, 1938

To S.S. and church. Miss Annie taught our class. Everyone was so happy to have Charles back. No one happier than I.

Did not go anywhere this afternoon. To church tonight. Willard and James Cash came over and played with Charles all afternoon.

Monday, October 10, 1938

Charles enrolled at the school house this morning. He knows that Hud is not coming for him and he is hurt and tries not to show it.

I stopped by the post office and mailed my letter to Hud. Then I went home to do the washing and ironing and to prepare Charles a proper room.

Miss Myrtle said that she doesn't know if she can stay here with a child in the house since she is around them all day. I assured her that Charles is no trouble and we will all get along.

Tuesday, October 11, 1938

Went to the bank this morning and made my deposit for the rent I've collected and the work I've done. A healthy sum it is and I feel better.

Lee Graham called and said that she was sending a man over who was interested in boarding with me, but I told her that Charles was home so she did not send him.

Washed four more quilts for Mrs. Hosick today. They are too heavy to get to the line now but Charles helped me. My boy is such a sweet blessing.

Wednesday, October 12, 1938

Brother Cash wants the women of the church to prepare an oyster supper next Monday for the stewards so we all met at Mrs. Hosick's to discuss it and make our plans.

Charles was out of school today for Columbus Day and Baby came as usual this morning.

Thursday, October 13, 1938

Miss Myrtle Henderson had an attack of appendicitis today. Mable came from the court house and carried her to the hospital in Chattanooga. Tonight she is better. She came home late this afternoon.

The orchestra played at some kind of meeting at Mrs. Rhyne's and Charles could not play because of his arm. But otherwise he enjoyed it.

Friday, October 14, 1938

Just the usual routine. Baby came as usual today. I get so tired so easy nowadays. Mary Elizabeth constantly reminds me that she's with me.

Saturday, October 15, 1938

Mable and Hattie went to Chattanooga this afternoon. Miss Myrtle is resting in her room. Charles and I baked cookies. Mable came home on the 4:45 bus from Chattanooga.

CHAPTER 21

Sunday, October 16, 1938

What a sad day it is! To S.S. this morning but I did not stay for church. Dr. and Mrs. Winslow lost their only child during the still hours of the morning. Hattie had stayed in Chattanooga and the roadster that Dr. Winslow had bought her was hit by a train as she was crossing Market Street. She was killed instantly.

I prayed for forgiveness tonight for the ill thoughts that I've held in my heart and in my mind for Hattie Winslow. She was only a few years older than me and I can now understand her being smitten with K.C. and my jealousy has subsided. Mable is heartbroken.

Monday, October 17, 1938

Our S.S. class served an oyster supper to the stewards of the church tonight. They seemed to enjoy it and we enjoyed preparing it. Hattie Winslow lies a corpse over at Hosick's and we went over there after the supper. Her coffin was not open.

Tuesday, October 18, 1938

Went to the bank this morning and then to Hattie's funeral this afternoon. Such a sweet funeral. Mable and I talked and I told her that it was pure Providence that she had not been in the car with her. And she told me that Hattie had wanted to go out to a night club and Mable didn't want to so she came on home. She said that Hattie had probably gone by herself and could not hold her drink. She said if she had gone with Hattie she'd probably be alive today, but I told her that she too could be just as dead. I promised Mable that I would not reveal our talk to Dr. or Mrs. Winslow. Hattie was really a good person.

Charles went to the fairgrounds awhile tonight. I enjoyed resting and reading. Miss Myrtle is better.

Wednesday, October 19, 1938

Baby came as usual this morning. We had our coffee, and she told me that Mable has been getting pretty thick with Georgia Turner's husband. I guess he's lonely since Georgia and the baby passed.

I listened quietly to Baby's sweet strains of "Go Tell Aunt Rhody" as she left by the back door to go make her rounds.

School had only one session today because of the fair, Miss Myrtle told me. Charles and I went to prayer meeting tonight. I pray and pray and pray.

Thursday, October 20, 1938

Miss Henderson and Charles are home early from school again because of the fair. Charles has gone to the fair this afternoon. I do not think I will go. I have to take care of myself if I'm to keep able to do the work. It is cold enough for a fire tonight.

Friday, October 21, 1938

Mable and Edsel Turner and Helen and William have gone to a donkey ball game at Trion tonight. Charles went to the fair again tonight. I have not been feeling well at all this week but am feeling better tonight.

Saturday, October 22, 1938

Madge Massey and two of her friends ran in for a few minutes—was glad to see them. They came to see Mable but she was not here. Charles has gone to the fair again.

Tonight I have enjoyed preparing a talk for S.S. tomorrow. May God bless the efforts!

Sunday, October 23, 1938

To S.S. and church today. Madge's sister, Susan, came down early after Charles and me and took us up home this afternoon. Baby, Maude and Tom were at Papa's. I was glad to get to go.

K.C. has been gone for four months. The passage of time has not lessened the pain of this whole ordeal. My sleep is so fitful and my sorrow deep.

Monday, October 24, 1938

Went over to Emily's this afternoon. She is not well. I did not go to the Circle meeting this evening. The nights are cold now.

Tuesday, October 25, 1938

I went to the bank this morning and then over to Emily's as I was needed. Little Joe is sick. Emily is right sick.

Wednesday, October 26, 1938

Baby told me this morning that Papa and Mr. Spencer have finally closed their land trade. I am so glad for Papa to get that off his mind. He worries too much.

I went to Chattanooga this afternoon with Emily. She is feeling better. I held

Little Joe while she drove. As we crossed Market Street, I could not help but think of poor Hattie Winslow not yet a week cold in her grave

Mable fixed supper for her, Miss Myrtle and Charles tonight and then she dropped Charles off at the show.

Miss Myrtle and I went to Prayer meeting tonight.

Thursday, October 27, 1938

Have been very busy today. I took Charles to Dr. Warrenfells to have the cast removed from his arm. He gave me more powder for my headache.

Washed this afternoon and mended some shirts for Edsel Turner. I didn't want pay but he insisted and gave me 35¢. Have lots of good literature to read if Mary Elizabeth will settle down long enough to let me. May God direct me.

Friday, October 28, 1938

Just the usual work today. Did not go anywhere. Miss Myrtle worked one session of school and then went to the fair at Summerville this afternoon.

Saturday, October 29, 1938

Baby was here as usual today. She is such a precious girl! And I am sure that she works too hard. Did not get to study my S.S. lesson today, but will try tonight.

Sunday, October 30, 1938

To S.S. and church this morning. Nowhere this afternoon. Oliver and Lee came after church and ate dinner with us. It was the 5th Sunday Union meeting of the Young People. The services were at the Methodist church.

Monday, October 31, 1938

Mable said that she and Edsel Turner have broken up. She says he was getting too fresh, but I suspect it's something else.

Mrs. Hosick and I took Charles to the Halloween carnival at the Grammar School tonight. On the way we dropped off Lee Graham's wash.

Tuesday, November 1, 1938

I washed today but did not get to the ironing. Bending is getting to be a chore. I want to go to the Presbyterian church tonight if I can.

Went to church. The man, Rev. Hammermill, is a missionary to China. He is very good.

Wednesday, November 2, 1938

I was quite surprised today when Maude came down. She just spent the day. I enjoyed her so much. She went back on the 4:25 bus. Charles and I went to the Presbyterian church again to hear Rev. Hammermill. He is very good.

Thursday, November 3, 1938

Went to church today. The Glory of it all! The Rev. E.H. Hammermill, missionary to China, is truly God's servant. His messages are very inspiring. To church tonight. Charles and Mable did not go.

Friday, November 4, 1938

We had a real hard rain this afternoon. Mr. Cobb and Walter picked up Charles and me in their roadster and drove us to church tonight.

Saturday, November 5, 1938

Miss Myrtle caught a ride with Mable and Helen to Chattanooga this afternoon. Charles and I went to church this evening and stopped to see Mrs. Rhyne on the way home. Julianna fell a few days ago and fractured her shoulder.

Sunday, November 6, 1938

Today's writing is found on page for Tuesday, Nov. 8. Made a mistake and turned two pages. Tuesday's writing is on this page.

Did a big washing today and ironed part of the things. Will get to the rest tonight.

Went to see how Emily and Little Joe are getting along.

Monday, November 7, 1938

Went to the W.M.S. this afternoon. Madge told me that Lee Graham had told her that Eva Smith's brother, Edgar Cannon, was coming home from New York. She said that it was because he had heard on the radio that Martians had invaded the planet! How absurd! Germans maybe. Madge said that if Edgar had been closer to his Almighty God and unwavering in his faith, he would have known that such things are impossible. It is true. The Devil beguiles the weak. I know.

While Baby was here this afternoon, she said that Aunt Ellen is in Erlanger Hospital with appendicitis. She said that her condition has gotten worse.

Tuesday, November 8, 1938

To S.S. today, but left my own church and went to hear the Rev. Hammermill again at the Presbyterian church. Went to the Week of Prayer program this afternoon.

Again tonight I left my own church, though I knew that Dr. Pierce was preaching his final sermon, and went to hear Mr. Hammermill. He is such a handsome man.

I made a mistake and turned two pages. This should have been on Sunday's page.

Wednesday, November 9, 1938

Baby said that she went to Erlanger yesterday and Aunt Ellen is better, but she is still sick. The appendix ruptured before she left home.

Today Charles and I moved the dining room where the bedroom has always been. Think I'll like the new arrangement better. Went to Prayer meeting tonight.

Thursday, November 10, 1938

Uncle J.C. called me this morning. He said Aunt Ellen is worse and wanted me to get word to Papa and Baby. I tried to call but could not reach them and just barely had time to get the bus and went up home. Papa was depressed and did not want to go to Erlanger to see his baby sister die. Baby and I went and Tom and Maude were there. Maude said that the doctor said that Aunt Ellen had a reaction and the crisis was passing and that maybe she will get better.

CHAPTER 22

Friday, November 11, 1938

The usual Friday's work. I baked a cake for Charles after dinner.

Saturday, November 12, 1938

Baby came as usual today. I feel so tired. She said that Papa said the way my stomach looks these days is like a pumpkin hanging on a door knob. I don't think he meant for her to tell me.

Since Rev. Hammermill left, I have not read much today, nor in several days.

Sunday, November 13, 1938

To S.S. and church today. Charles played with Walter Cobb today all afternoon. I went for the mail after dinner. I hoped for some word from Hud but I really did not expect it.

Lee Graham picked me up in front of the house and took me for a ride. We went out to Mineral Springs awhile. She said Oliver was not home.

Monday, November 14, 1938

The Mission Study class met at Mrs. Hosick's but I did not try to go. I don't feel real well. Charles has gone on an outing with the children who had a contest during the Baptist Revival.

Tuesday, November 15, 1938

This has turned out to be a beautiful day! I washed and my clothes dried so nicely. I am reading "Life By Faith" by Colbert W. Cross and the China Inland Mission. It is fine reading.

Did not iron today. My back hurts too much. Mable and Miss Myrtle took Charles to Chattanooga to see the Dionne quintuplets at the theater.

Wednesday, November 16, 1938

It has rained all day. Papa had his hogs killed yesterday. Baby said she had a colored woman to help her with the lard. I know they have had an awful time today for the rain has not ceased.

Mable has gone somewhere tonight. No prayer meeting tonight because of the Annual Conference.

Thursday, November 17, 1938

Everyone went somewhere tonight and I was planning such a delightful time of study and prayer when Mrs. Hosick came over for about an hour. Then in less than half an hour Mable came home and I was alone for only a few minutes after all. No time alone for practice or prayer.

I am trying to plan a devotion for the Mission Study class tomorrow afternoon.

Friday, November 18, 1938

Went to the Mission Study class at Emily's this afternoon. Gave the devotion.

Saturday, November 19, 1938

Disappointed again tonight. No chance to read or pray. Charles and the violin students went to Rome today with Mrs. Rhyne to some kind of musical meeting and banquet. He enjoyed it very much. It is turning colder tonight. Am glad for the rain to cease for awhile.

Sunday, November 20, 1938

To S.S. this morning. No services at our church because of the Annual Conference. Charles and I went up home on the twelve o'clock bus. Maude and Tom and Uncle Jack Clifford and Aunt Ellen were there. So were Baby and Papa. I was glad to see all of them. We all enjoyed being there. Baby brought us back. To the Presbyterian church tonight.

Monday, November 21, 1938

Went to Emily's for awhile this afternoon. Little Joe is getting so big. He does not cry like he did at first.

Tuesday, November 22, 1938

Washed today. Read this afternoon. Everyone gone somewhere tonight except Charles and myself.

Wednesday, November 23, 1938

Papa is sick. Baby said this morning he was sick all night. Seems to have an upset stomach. Then this afternoon she called me from Sid's Service Station and said she had called Dr. Warrenfells. He was out and did not get in until about dark. I talked to him. He said his temperature is 101 and he is delirious at times. But doesn't think he is dangerous.

My beloved [C!] has been gone five months now. I am too tired to cry.

Thursday, November 24, 1938

Thanksgiving day. Am having hen for dinner. I invited no one but Emily's family because Miss Myrtle is here. It is a cold, rainy, snowy morning. Am anxious about Papa.

Went up there on the 9:30 bus and Mable and Bob Davis came for me about eleven.

Friday, November 25, 1938

Papa is better. Went to Mrs. Hosick's a little while this morning. Went to Emily's this afternoon and we went to see Sadie Richard this afternoon. She had her tonsils removed a few days ago.

Saturday, November 26, 1938

Miss Myrtle got a ride with Mable to Chattanooga early this morning and has been gone all day. Had the hot water disconnected today. It is turning colder. The hot water side was frozen this morning.

Sunday, November 27, 1938

To S.S. but did not stay for church. Came home to cook dinner. I did not go anywhere this afternoon. James and Willard came to play with Charles.

Went to church tonight. It is turning colder.

Monday, November 28, 1938

Went up home on the 9:30 bus this morning. Was coming home on the eleven o'clock bus, but while I was waiting Dr. Warrenfells came by and I got a ride to town.

Tuesday, November 29, 1938

It was so cold today. I did not try to wash. Anyway Baby did not get to come yesterday with her things. But I'll do them as soon as she needs them.

Wednesday, November 30, 1938

Baby came as usual today. I did the washing this afternoon. Charles is such a precious heart. He filled the wash tubs for me and also carried the wash to the line. To prayer meeting tonight.

Thursday, December 1, 1938

Got my clothes all dried and ironed today. Charles delivered all the laundry for me before he went to the show tonight. I will collect for it later.

Mable is out somewhere with Bob Davis, I'm sure. Miss Myrtle and I are alone tonight.

Friday, December 2, 1938

I did a big day's work today. House cleaning, etc. Charles helped me put the stove up in Miss Myrtle's room.

Mable and Helen went to Chattanooga. All is quiet after dinner. Miss Myrtle has gone 'possum hunting tonight.

Saturday, December 3, 1938

Bob Davis ate supper with us today. He and Mable have gone to a dance tonight. Gladys paid me $5.28 for teaching Betty Allen last summer. I was glad to get it and surely appreciated it.

Sunday, December 4, 1938

Mable's birthday. I invited some of her friends to eat supper with us. Bob Davis, Helen and William, Emily and Tommy and Little Joe, and Oliver and Lee were there. Madge dropped by. It wasn't the same without Hattie.

Went to S.S. and church as usual. Charles and Walter Cobb went home with James and Willard after church and Walter and Mr. Cobb brought him home.

Mrs. Hosick came over for awhile this afternoon. To church tonight.

Monday, December 5, 1938

Went to W.M.S. at Mrs. Hosick's this afternoon. The discussion was about baskets for Christmas. I was not sitting comfortably, not that I can anymore. It was so good to get back home where I could rest.

Tuesday, December 6, 1938

Had a good chance to read and study and rest today. Mary Elizabeth is taking her toll on me. This year has been almost more than I can take. So much change and upheaval.

Wednesday, December 7, 1938

Did the washing today. I can do it no longer. Dear Charles is such a help but he is having to carry more and more of the burden. I told him that from now until Mary Elizabeth is born we will only be doing wash for the family. I'll let everyone know the next few days.

To Prayer meeting tonight. The League had charge of the services tonight. The interruption came when Mrs. Peacock told us that Mrs. Hugh Don Center's house had caught fire and had burned to the ground. She was devastated. They lost all of their belongings.

CHAPTER 23

Thursday, December 8, 1938

Mable worked at the courthouse today. I have had telephone calls from neighbors concerning the wash. They are all so very kind and understanding. Charles is going with me to collect the last of my pay. Mable is out somewhere tonight.

Friday, December 9, 1938

Mable worked again today. I finished my ironing this afternoon.

Saturday, December 10, 1938

Just the usual work today except I finished up Edsel Turner's shirts. He came by for them before supper. Lucile and her children were here from Cloudland visiting. It pains me to see her.

Did not get to study my S.S. lesson until after ten o'clock. Studied from 10:00 to 11:15.

Sunday, December 11, 1938

To S.S. and church today. The new Presiding Elder preached. I liked his sermon.

Did not go anywhere until late this afternoon. I went over to the cemetery as cold as it was to ponder my thoughts and have a good cry. It is so cold and lonely there and that is what I deserve.

This year is almost over and I am so happy to see it go. It seems that they don't get any better. To church tonight to pray.

Monday, December 12, 1938

Went up home on the twelve o'clock bus while I still can. They are getting along all right. Baby was going to bring me back, but Maude borrowed her car to come to LaFayette so I came with her.

Tuesday, December 13, 1938

Have some orders for books ready to mail. Am making note of it so I'll know when I ordered it. "In the Clouds." Gist of the Lesson. L.B.R.A. Literature Biblical Research Society.

Wednesday, December 14, 1938

The Orchestra played for the American Legion this afternoon. To Prayer meeting tonight.

Thursday, December 15, 1938

Baby was here for a few minutes this afternoon. She came to town to see about getting her a new stove. She told me that Minnie Turner, Edsel's mother, fell on the ice yesterday and broke her hip. She is in Erlanger Hospital.

Miss Myrtle, Mable and Charles have gone to the Christmas cantata at the church. I did not feel up to it. I am alone. Hope I am not too tired to read to my heart's content.

Friday, December 16, 1938

The weather is not appropriate to go out and about. Everyone is home tonight. Mable made some cocoa for everyone. I could not drink any. I went to bed early.

Saturday, December 17, 1938

Mary Elizabeth is a very active child. Many times today I could not stay on my feet and had to sit down.

It is snowing hard and we are all staying in the house. Miss Myrtle and Charles brought home a Christmas tree. Mable made some more cocoa. She popped some corn to string on the tree. The smell is making me nauseated.

Sunday, December 18, 1938

Mable, Charles and Miss Myrtle walked to S.S. and church this morning.

I did not go. The Christmas cantata is being held again tonight and I didn't go to that either.

Monday, December 19, 1938

The Circle met this afternoon but I did not go. My legs are swollen.

Tuesday, December 20, 1938

The snow has melted some but it is still cold today. Have not done much, but the ordinary work. Everyone seems to be making their plans for Christmas.

School closed today. Miss Myrtle went home on the eleven o'clock bus.

Wednesday, December 21, 1938

Did not go to Prayer meeting tonight. Stayed home by the fire.

Thursday, December 22, 1938

Emily and Little Joe visited me awhile this afternoon. She brought me some more baby things for Mary Elizabeth.

Friday, December 23, 1938

Ravanell and Ned came in from Florida tonight. It is good to see them. It has been so long. So much to catch up on what with Judge's house now belonging to Mr. Hosick. Mable and Bob went out somewhere tonight. She was so surprised to see Ravanell when she got back. It seems our little family has pulled back together somehow, even if it is only briefly.

[C!] has been gone six months. It seems like only yesterday. I find it difficult to collect my thoughts.

Saturday, December 24, 1938

Charles and Walter are having a good time with their firecrackers tonight. Charles gets a bicycle this Christmas. He always has to ride Walter Cobb's so I made sure he would have his own this year. I never could convince Judge that boys need bicycles to ride on their adventures. He always thought that I indulged Charles too much, but Charles is such a good boy and I know that he is worth it.

We are all going up home to Papa's in the morning. Maude is fixing dinner. Mable and Bob and Ravanell and Ned are out somewhere.

Sunday, December 25, 1938

Such a pleasant day Maude cooked dinner and Tom went to Huntsville and carried Mrs. Shields back so she could eat dinner with us. Charles and I rode up home with Mable and Bob Davis and Ned and Ravanell drove their car. Charles had left early this morning for S.S. but left as soon as the classes assembled so he will not be counted absent. Madge came over for awhile this afternoon. Charles has been riding his bicycle all evening. To vespers tonight.

* * *

Monday, December 26, 1938

The water was frozen this morning. It started raining after dinner. Turned to snow late tonight.

Tuesday, December 27, 1938

Charles and Walter rode up home on their bicycles to Rock Spring today. It is very cold but they made the trip all right. They were back a little before two.

Emily said Little Joe is sick again and she is not getting out with him. Ned and Ravanell have been gone visiting family and friends.

It is much colder. Charles gathered the firewood in for me.

CHAPTER 24

Wednesday, December 28, 1938

The sorrow of all sorrows! The world is no more a pleasant place! Baby did not come this morning and I didn't get worried until around dinner. I called all over and no one had seen her.

About 9:15 tonight the searchers found her. Her milk truck had slid on the ice in a curve and left the roadway and struck a boulder. My beloved Baby was thrown through the windshield onto the rocky bank of the Chickamauga.

O! My heart is broken! My dear sweet Baby lying broken and bleeding on the rocks. An artery in her arm was severed and she lay on the rocks, cold and alone, with her very life blood seeping out to the icy water.

[See opposite page] [December 28, 1938]

Thursday, December 29, 1938

It pains me to think of me sitting in my nice warm house close to the fire and my precious Baby lying on the cold rocks dying alone in the snow. No one saw her down the embankment and her calls for help were in vain.

O, God! My dear Clydellen is no more. She was my rock and my redeemer; the soother of my soul! O, what is to become of me without darling Baby? I can't go on without her. My grief is more than I can bear. [Dec. 29] This is a rainy day. It is dark and bleak and the dead of winter. Not a sign of life is to be found. I can't stop crying. Maude is beside herself and Papa cannot be consoled.

Friday, December 30, 1938

Clydellen Orenduff, my beloved Baby sister, was buried today. She was twenty-five years old. It was such a sweet funeral. We are all still in shock of the situation. The entire community is stunned. We always heard that John Thomas Brinkman was sweet on Baby, but I never knew for sure until I saw him at the funeral. His tears were flowing unrestrained, as did ours. The singing was sweet and they also sang Baby's favorite song, "Go Tell Aunt Rhody."

Maude is staying with Papa tonight. My mind is numb. My head feels as if it's filled with cotton. I don't know how to cope with all of this. I am alone in the dark tonight.

Saturday, December 31, 1938

Everyone is gone today. Charles is staying with Walter Cobb and Ravanell and Ned are over at Ned's granny's. Mable and Bob are in Chattanooga to a New Year's Eve Party at the Choo Choo, I believe.

Mary Elizabeth and I are alone. Little did I know when I began this journal that this year would be so upsetting and bring so much tragedy. Little did I know that my precious Baby would not see 1939.

My sin and desperation have multiplied this year and my conscience robs me of sleep. I cannot go on. The burden and punishment are too great to bear. It is time to atone for my sins so that I may be right with Jesus. The world is so much against me. I must—

Here the diary ended and Cathy stared at the page for what seemed an eternity. Disbelief gave way to shock, and that to anger. Sitting bolt upright this time, she read the page over and over, as though the ending would jump from its hiding place and make itself known to her. *What in the hell is this! She can't end it like this!* Cathy's thoughts screamed inside her head.

She sank back on her pillows and tried to reason it all out. Maybe Lynette, in her desperation, had committed suicide. Maybe she confessed and K.C. Fox had been found and the police had come to arrest her. Maybe....

The sun was not yet up when Cathy fell into deep slumber, her dreams haunting her with images of

Lynette, Mable, Charles, K.C. Fox, and Baby. Cathy watched in slow motion as the shovel came crashing down on K.C. Fox's skull, leaving him limp and lifeless, as a sock puppet thrown into a child's toy box, on the floor of Miss Mary Lizzie's garden shed. Slow motion showed her the terrified look on Hattie Winslow's face as she realized that she had made a mistake in trying to beat the train across Market Street, and the ultimate carnage that had been visited upon her as rescuers worked feverishly to pry her from the wreckage.

Baby haunted her dreams, too, and Cathy felt cold in her bones as she watched the milk truck slide into the curve and plummet over the embankment, its journey impeded by a large boulder, immediately sending Baby crashing through the windshield onto the rocky bank of the creek.

Cathy imagined that the gravity of Baby's plight brought on an agony of pain and realization as her warm blood spread until it was a barely perceptible sensation on her skin. She had had no time to be afraid, the damage being inflicted swiftly. The battered and broken body could only moan, as Death did not take her instantly, yet she knew the severity of what was inevitable, and time took on no meaning. As Lynette had so described, Baby's very life blood drained slowly from her body and mingled with the icy waters of the Chickamauga.

* * *

The ensuing week had been filled with all work and no Harry, who had returned from California, only to make a run to Texas, and she had to settle for what she called "marriage by phone." To fill the void, her free hours were spent making phone calls and conducting computer research, following up leads and crashing into dead ends.

Her web searches entertained her with historical aspects of life in 1938. She became immersed in the stories of the times, such as Nazi Germany and Hitler's maniacal leadership, Pre-World War II clothing articles that portrayed the styles of 1938 with a much softer look than the business attire of the forties, stories of "every man." She even found a site about Clarence Darrow, the defense attorney in the famed "Scopes Monkey Trial."

In 1925, the State of Tennessee had enacted legislation that would make it a crime for evolution to be taught in public schools, and John Scopes, a science teacher and part-time football coach, was arrested and charged with the crime. The trial took place in Dayton, Tennessee, not far from Chattanooga, Cathy noted, and she thought that someday she might visit the town where William Jennings Bryan and Clarence Darrow battled for victory.

Scopes was ultimately found guilty and fined one hundred dollars, and Darrow welcomed the opportunity for appeal. Bryan succumbed to heart failure in Dayton six days after the trial, however, Darrow had died in 1938.

Cathy's computer table was covered with piles of notes scribbled on the backs of scrap paper and old bills. Her lists were growing longer and she followed up leads until they had exhausted themselves in the archives of antiquity. She would fall into bed, her energy spent, no closer than she had been.

Every night since discovering the diary and its contents, the odious visions came back to her again and again. Sometimes, they sounded in her ears like the whoosh and pounding of complex machinery or the distant passage of a train over a worn-out railroad trestle. During these times, she would feel night sweats, and pant as though she were suffocating, as though her blood would not properly circulate. She tried to read something else, but it was in vain, as her thoughts continually went back to the day of the murder, and she would go through it each night in all its most secret details with Lynette and all of the violent emotions that she had experienced.

Cathy would wake with a sense of fear and dread, exhausted from her travels in dream time. *These people are all dead now, but somebody needs to know. Judge Stinson and K.C. Fox were victims of a woman whom they had both victimized, and no one knew.* Despite her strong desire to find out the fate of Lynette, who had opened a portal to a simpler, and at the same time, more complex segment of human existence, Cathy weighed the consequences of sharing this information with the local authorities. *Whether or not they had deserved it, people just don't get away with murder!*

Cathy considered their descendants and the sensation that this kind of news story would cause in such a small town. Judge's body would probably be exhumed, and the millpond would have to be drained, that is, if the authorities believed her. If the diary were made public, even more than seventy years after the fact, many lives would be affected and changed forever. She needed to talk to Harry. He would know the right thing to do, so until then, she decided to do nothing.

* * *

When her shift ended on Friday night, she and Gigi exchanged good-byes in the darkening shadows. Fred picked up Gigi and the two waited in the parking lot until Cathy was safe in her car before driving away. As the engine was warming, Cathy discovered that she had left her cigarette case in the pocket of her lab coat in the locker room, so she turned off the car and went back inside the building.

Thoughts about the diary had been nagging her all day: Papa, the milk truck, and millpond. They had sounded all too familiar, and suddenly it occurred to her that she *had* heard these things before she had read them in the diary. She hastily punched the elevator button and went upstairs to the second floor.

Mr. Mack was sitting up in his chair as Wendy was trying to feed him. He looked up at Cathy and a fleeting smile came to his lips.

"Need any help?" Cathy ventured.

"Yes!" came Mr. Mack's definite reply.

"Now, Mr. Mack," Wendy chided.

"It's okay, Wendy. I'll help him, if you want. Mr. Mack and I are old friends, right, Mr. Mack?"

"I 'spose so," he muttered.

"All right, then," Wendy replied, "I'll check on the others. I'll be across the hall if you need anything."

Cathy settled in before Mr. Mack, and she picked up his fork and surveyed his meal. "Well," she began, "meatloaf might not be so bad."

"Hmph!" he snorted.

"What do you like to eat?" Cathy asked him, genuinely.

"I think my fav'rit's just about swee' 'tator pie," he smiled at her.

I can probably make a pretty good sweet potato pie," Cathy reassured him, "But, it's probably not going to be as good as your mother's."

"Prob'ly not," he nodded.

"I'll make one and sneak it in here to you. Would you like that?"

He smiled curiously, still nodding his head. "That would be right nice. Why would you go to all that bother for an ol' man like me?"

"Because I like you, Mr. Mack. And, I respect you."

"Why? I ain't never done nothin' fo' you."

"If for no other reason, Mr. Mack, I do respect your age. You've made it further than I have, and I imagine that you know a lot more about life than I do." Her calm expression seemed to put Mr. Mack at ease, and he no longer eyed her suspiciously.

"I didn't know white folks thought like that."

"Believe it or not, Mr. Mack, some of us do."

"Sit with me awhile? I think I'm ready to eat now."

"Gladly, sir," she smiled, "Do you care if we talk while you eat your dinner?"

"Suits me fine."

"You were telling me the other day," she began, as she cut a piece of meatloaf and held it up to his lips, "about when you were a teenager in LaFayette, and a judge gave you and your cousin a year in jail for making moonshine."

"Yep," he shook his head. "That's me an' Thad."

"Do you remember the judge's name?"

"Never fo'git it...Stinson," came the sad reply as he spat, "Mean bastard."

A shiver went up Cathy's spine, as this revelation lent credence to the diary, and the notion of its reality was sinking in. She decided to test his memory.

"How long did you live in LaFayette?"

"Sev'ral years; left there in '41, when I married a girl from Chatt'nooga. That's when I moved up here. It didn't work out, but I stayed."

"What happened to Thad?"

"Oh, he left LaFayette long fo' I did. Said he didn't want no part of no hangin' judge. Think he finally settled 'round Atlanta."

Cathy chose her words carefully, so as not to make Mr. Mack distrustful or uneasy. "Did you ever hear of a man named K.C. Fox?"

"Name sounds familiar, but I don't rightly rec'lect."

"Do you know what the judge's daughter's name was? Mable?"

"That's fo' sure, Miss Mable," he laughed, confidently. "She's a toot fo' sure. Liked the gentlemens a lot. Dated a lot in town and in Chatt'nooga. One summer night, I's workin' down at the Lake, pickin' up trash and what not, and I come upon Miss Mable and Mr. Marcus behind some garbage cans really goin' at it. Man, oh, man, if them garbage cans could talk. What stories they could tell. Don't know if Miz Trammel eve' found out, though," he laughed heartily at the memory, as though he were reminiscing with an old friend.

Wide-eyed, Cathy asked, "Did they see you?"

"Hell, no! I got outta there quick. I didn't want to go to no jail again!"

She and Mr. Mack shared quite a bit of merriment of this recollection. Cathy lifted a spoonful of applesauce to Mr. Mack's lips and he ate appreciatively. She felt fortunate to have made Mr. Mack's acquaintance, and felt that their meeting at this point in time was kismet. His softer and gentler side was grandfatherly and comforting, and she greatly admired the beauty of his calm simplicity with Life.

"What about someone named Baby?"

Mr. Mack expelled more hearty laughter. "Whew! Lord have mercy! That's a name I ain't heard in ages! Miss Baby Orenduff!"

"You knew her?" Cathy was excited and hoped her trembling did not show.

"Oh, yeah," he laughed, shaking his head, "Miss Baby was a fine woman. My sister, Vena, used to work fo' her up to th' dairy."

"She ran a dairy?"

"Well, it wuz Mr. Clyde's dairy, and Miss Baby, she drove th' milk truck. She was the one what come down to the mill to pick up th' moon, and then she'd take it out with her on deliveries. Mr. Clyde was kind of gruff, but, Miss Baby, well, she wuz a good sort. Always treated me real nice. Always bringin' us somethin' to eat down to th' mill. Blackberry pie, I believe. Thad thought highly of her, too. We'd always help out Miss Baby if'n we could." He gazed toward the window, sadly reliving the moment.

"Are you all right, Mr. Mack?"

He shook his head, affirmatively. "I's just thinkin' what happened to Miss Baby."

"What happened to her?" Cathy felt that she should ask the question even though she already knew the answer. After all, it seemed natural, and it would give Mr. Mack the opportunity to vent his emotion of the incident.

"Seems like right after Christmas, don't exactly

remember what year...Miss Baby had a wreck in her milk truck. Throwed her clean through the windshield. Cut her up pretty bad." His outstretched arm cut through the air. "Didn't kill her right away though. She laid out there on the creek bank in the snow til she finally bled to death. Nobody there to help her." He wiped his watery eyes with the back of his gnarled hand.

"You really liked Miss Baby, didn't you?"

"Yeah," he sniffed, "We all did. Miss Baby wuz one of a kind. Knew how to treat people. Always concerned about somebody else. Always helpin' others...and in her time of need, the Lord saw fit fo' her to go it alone. And, that's what she did."

"Did you know any of Miss Baby's sisters?"

"Naw, didn't know much about the fambly, but I think one of 'em was married to that hangin' judge. Vena knowed 'em all better'n I did."

"Where is Vena now?" she inquired.

"Oh, she died sev'ral years back. The cancer took her."

"I'm sorry," Cathy proffered, and she was genuinely sorry that he had lost his sister, and she was sorry that she had lost another lead. She noticed that as they had talked, his meal was almost consumed. "Do you want anymore?"

"No, no thank you," he said, concisely, "Had plenty."

"Well," she rose from her chair, "I'll get out of your way and I'll go home and make a sweet potato pie this weekend and bring it to you when I come back. Would you like that?"

"Yes, I would, Miss Cathy," he smiled, "but, you don't have to go to no trouble for the likes of me. I'll be all right."

"It's no trouble," said Cathy, "not for a friend. I'd be happy to do it. I'll see you Monday, okay?"

"That'd be right fine," he nodded, appreciating that he had found a true friend.

CHAPTER 25

Saturday morning was crisp and scorching all at the same time. The northeast wind was fresh, and the thin overcast had already burned off. The world seemed vibrant and beautiful, yet Cathy had difficulty feeling connected to it. Cathy wondered if Lynette had taken advantage of these vibrant, beautiful autumn days, or had taken them for granted, her time spent washing, ironing, making cakes, and going to vespers.

Gigi called and invited her to a late lunch, and Cathy graciously accepted. She decided to feel Gigi out, as it were, to take her into her confidence, only telling her that which she wanted her to know. Many times she had been on the verge of revelation, but had lost her nerve. She valued Gigi's opinion, but sometimes, it came across like a saber's cutting edge. The progress of lunch would cue Cathy as to how much about Lynette she should reveal, and then she could gauge Gigi's reception of the diary's information.

They met downtown at a street cafe and chose a sidewalk table. Under an awning, they sat in a shadow that lay upon that side of the building, despite the sun blazing triumphantly out a serene sky. Across the street, a row of elms had been planted as part of an urban renewal project, as well as to reintroduce the dying species to the area. The day was bright, and the brilliant blue silhouetted the drooping boughs of the elms, and their leaves became colored, serrated spear points swaying in the light October breeze.

Gigi could not help but notice Cathy's distance, and they sat still for a while, perusing their lunch menus. The brightness of the morning was beginning to fade, and finally, exchanging lighthearted chitchat, they ordered their lunch. Doubt and hesitation showed on Cathy's face, and even though Gigi was curious, she acquiesced to the awkward prattle, and waited patiently. *Cathy smokes too much*. She thought this to be a ridiculous indulgence.

Cathy's uneasy thoughts seemed to be troubled and complex, and, faltering, she began her story. She told Gigi that she had found some old books and letters with Lynette's name in them and that she was curious about the woman, opting not to reveal the journal or its contents. Gigi listened attentively, not wanting to dampen the atmosphere, and suggested that it would be a lark to go to LaFayette to search out a family from 1938, having no idea of the gravity of the mission. Cathy smiled at her friend, genuinely grateful that Gigi would cooperate and render much needed assistance. After all, it was now Gigi's idea.

"Did you find these books and letters in that old chest Harry brought you?" Gigi inquired.

The question put Cathy on the spot, but she answered immediately, "Yes, and they seem to indicate that this woman lived in LaFayette. I thought it might be amusing to maybe find her or some of her family...and return the books to them. Even if we don't find them, it will be an adventure," she continued reassuringly, as she opened a fresh package of salad wafers, and appropriated a bottle of Italian dressing from a nearby table.

"Get the salt, too," Gigi ordered and Cathy complied.

"This is going to be fun," Gigi returned, "Hmmmm, this sandwich is good. And today is gorgeous."

As they ate their club sandwiches and salads, Cathy tried to imagine what downtown Chattanooga had looked like when Mable and Hattie had sported around, but, somehow, her visionary faculties failed to cooperate. They could have even ridden in Hattie's roadster down this very same street on a day much like today, just as Cathy and Gigi had done, separated only by time and space.

As they ate, Cathy offered bits and pieces of information in the diary, so when they arrived in Walker County, Gigi could be on the lookout. She also told her about the recent conversation with Mr. Mack and suggested that maybe they could look up some of his "old friends." Gigi was amicable to these suggestions, and was actually quite satisfied to get out of the city, if even for a few hours.

After lunch, Cathy paid the check and they drove to LaFayette. Gigi noticed a marked change in her friend's manner, and an eight-years' friendship had taught her when a boot-up of the "old rancid" was called for, and when she should just sit and listen. Now, however, she noticed that Cathy seemed to be more at ease, and her sisterly demeanor was returning. Cathy's age, Gigi knew, lay somewhere on the sunny side of forty, and unlike her own, did not seek and expect to win admiration, even long after the average woman would cease to be considered attractive. But, Gigi found a matronly attractiveness about Cathy that she admired greatly.

Gigi felt, however, that anyone endowed with such a temperament as her own, would be as a rule, unreasonably jealous of youth and good looks in another. Yet, she could not decide if Cathy's attitude toward her were to be ascribed to complacency, or self-satisfaction, or to a nobler motive. At least, Cathy gave her no hint of jealousy, and Gigi was sufficed with Cathy's unfeigned joy at spending her time and sharing her company.

Cathy decided to travel by way of Chickamauga Battlefield; a nice drive with October's beauty and splendor, the exploding colors of the turning leaves and the serenity of the battlefield, itself. The winding black ribbon of asphalt was flanked by woods and fields, raw in their beauty, but giving the appearance of constant attention. Monuments, representing the states whose troops had fought and died there, gave mute testimony to the carnage that had taken place.

Chickamauga Battlefield was the site of one of the Civil War's most climactic battles between Union General William S. Rosecrans and Confederate General Braxton Bragg, which had lasted three days, killing or wounding almost 35, 000 soldiers, the Confederacy victorious. Chickamauga, the creek and the town, were named a Native American word meaning "Stagnant River," but after the fighting had ended, it would be better known as the "River of Death." Knowing little about the area's history, Gigi listened attentively as Cathy shared these bits of historical knowledge with her.

Even passing through Rock Spring, which was little more than a wide spot in the road, gave new meaning to the name on the sign. Cathy couldn't begin to imagine what this stretch of road had looked like in 1938, but it was not a large double-lane highway as she saw, and was sure that, decades ago, it had probably not even been paved. The thought of Charles and Walter Cobb riding their bicycles to Rock Spring and back instantly popped into her mind, and she mentally noted the reading on her odometer to see how far the community was located from LaFayette. Her eyes scanned the countryside in hopes of ascertaining where the Orenduff Dairy might have been, but too much time had passed, and landmarks had changed.

During the thirties, many projects had been completed, including roadwork, by Franklin Roosevelt's Civilian Conservation Corps by workers at Camp Booker T. Washington, located at The Pocket, and Camp Dick Russell at Lookout Mountain. Many poor Walker County boys had entered the camps with no money, no friends, and seemingly no future, and had observed and learned, and participated in restoring the nation's economy and beauty, according to President Roosevelt's plan. In return, they received thirty dollars each month, twenty-five of which was sent to their families.

As Chickamauga Battlefield had been the first proclaimed National Park, particular attention was afforded the Old Federal Road, which ran through the park, trickling down to adjacent areas in Chickamauga, Rock Spring, and LaFayette. Old LaFayette Road was one of the road projects, intersecting the Old Federal Road at intervals.

Cathy mentioned points of interest to Gigi as they traveled, yet she felt no affinity for this area so steeped in history, despite the tragedies of the past century. She found it difficult to feel a connection to it, and wondered if her feelings were failing her. Perhaps, she might even be taking her investigation in the wrong direction. However, she endeavored to find enjoyment in the explosive coloring of the autumn leaves, for she knew that as the weeks passed, by the end of the year, the tree branches would be barren of foliage, and what remained would be patches of washed out saffron and dismal rust.

Maybe, she could relate better to LaFayette, the county seat of Walker County. Prior to their outing, Cathy's computer research had revealed that the town was founded in the 1880s, and was named in honor of the French nobleman, Marquis Marie Joseph Yves Gilbert Du Motier LaFayette, who assisted America during the American Revolution. Despite its history, nothing jumped out at her, no guiding instinct, no validation.

As she drove in, she noticed the town square and wondered what Baby might have seen as she had driven in from Rock Spring, a few miles away. Gigi saw a sign in front of the public library and suggested that they start there. Cathy agreed and turned her car into the parking lot.

Once inside, the two were greeted by Miss Belva Hammond. The librarian was a lovely thin woman, small and gray, with the face of a mouse, who seemed more than willing to help them. Cathy did not mention the diary, but simply told her that she was doing some family research. Distant relatives and such.

"Books are like people," she imparted, "because they are graceful, amusing, and entertaining. Some books furnish pleasant companionship for a little while; others, because they are solid and dependable, and useful, are frequently called upon for help and advice. We speak of the latter, faithful helpers as reference books." She ran her hand lovingly across the spines of several volumes within her reach.

Behind her back, Gigi sighed, silently, and rolled her eyes. Cathy knew from years of friendship with Gigi, that this look meant that she thought that "Miss Hammond's train had left the tracks a long time ago."

Miss Hammond directed them to the Genealogy Room where Cathy and Gigi pored over microfilm that lent credence to the diary. As the microfilm machines whirred, to Gigi, they were perusing old Walker County newspapers, but each time that Cathy came across a name she recognized, it was as if she were reading about an old friend.

One particular corroboration caught her attention: Little Florene, seven months old, infant daughter of Edsel and Georgia Mae Turner succumbed to crib death last Wednesday. Cathy felt distressed as she read the short account of the baby's brief life, of which Little Florene had had no understanding, and her unexplainable death, which she had faced without fear, not having had the benefit of the realization of living. Then, she read the article about the suicide.

Gigi was amazed by some of the articles and the advertising. "Hey, Cat," she whispered gleefully, "You're not going to believe this, work shirts were $2.99! Beans were a nickel!"

Cathy smiled and nodded at her, absorbed in her own discoveries. A deep realization struck her as she read the caption under the picture of a local businessman. "Marcus Trammel."

She tried to recall where she had heard the name before. *Somebody had mentioned the name Marcus Trammel.*

Marcus Trammel. Trammel's Mill! Mr. Mack worked at Trammel's Mill!

Cathy searched the archives to the 1940s and found no mention of the murder of K.C. Fox. No mention of Lynette's death by suicide, or otherwise. As Cathy and Gigi prepared to leave, they stopped to express their appreciation to Miss Hammond for a few moments.

"Yes," she mused, "it seems that I do remember a Miss Mary Lizzie that lived over on Mulberry Street. But, she died when I was just a little girl. Mama took my sister, Frances, and me to the funeral."

"Frances Hammond? Your sister is Frances Hammond?" Cathy inquired.

"Yes, she used to be. She married a local boy, Eugene Cornett."

"Does she live here? Maybe, she knows what happened to Miss Lynette," Cathy masked her zeal with nonchalance. Hearing the names, she felt as though she were discussing the whereabouts of old neighbors whom she hadn't seen in years. In 1938, Charles had attended Frances Hammond's birthday party, and one of his friends had been Eugene Cornett. Between the two of them, their memories could possibly supply intricate pieces to this puzzle.

"No, I'm afraid not," Miss Hammond responded, sadly, "Frances and Eugene were killed in an automobile accident about fifteen years ago. They were driving back from Florida and made it as far as Whitfield. Their car left the roadway and overturned in Swamp Creek. Frances drowned and Eugene's neck was broken. So tragic, so tragic."

"I'm so sorry," Cathy offered, and her sorrow was heartfelt.

"Thank you, dear," Miss Hammond said, "I've missed them so."

How gracious Miss Hammond had been to them, and how charmingly she spoke of her impressions of literary engagement. By right of birth, she had been given something that Cathy felt that she, herself, had missed. She had been made privy to intimate glimpses up narrow streets and widened avenues, and had made the acquaintance of a prominent family on the heels of her older sister. Following their chat, the librarian proved to be very helpful and directed Cathy and Gigi to the next block, Mulberry Street, where they would find the Tyler-Hosick Funeral Home.

Cathy's pulse was racing as they thanked the woman and hurried out to her car. She felt her heart fluttering at this happy circumstance. *At last, Hosick Funeral Home!* She immediately felt as though she were making progress, and this new bit of information spurred her on. Spontaneously, she and Gigi had gasped, almost as though they had been thinking the same thoughts, but Cathy knew were entirely different reasons.

She rounded the block, pulled into the funeral home lot and parked her car. Taking a deep breath, she knew that the time had come to take Gigi into her confidence. Her story poured forth as a fine trickle of sand through a crystal hourglass, and Gigi delayed her comments until she was sure that Cathy had ceased her fervent phrasings.

Cathy did not reveal the details of the love triangle and the murders, but now Gigi knew of the diary and sat in awe of the revelation. The two quickly got their story straight so as not to raise suspicion among the locals. Gigi promised to listen intently, lest Cathy should miss something important.

Mrs. Tyler proved to be a very nice woman who was very interested in Cathy's quest and said that her family, the Hosicks, had lived in LaFayette and Walker County for generations. She went on to say that she had not personally known Judge Stinson's family, but she could show Cathy and Gigi the house where Judge's wife had lived after he died.

Cathy and Gigi looked at each other in disbelief. Gigi spoke first, "You mean the house is still standing?"

Cathy couldn't believe her ears. Mrs. Tyler walked them to the parking lot and then pointed to a dilapidated, ochre house across the street. The wraparound porch sagged in places, its two-story grandeur having been left in an earlier decade.

"My grandpa bought the judge's house after the judge died back in the thirties," Mrs. Tyler told Cathy, "but, it burned down during the winter of '51, I believe. Mama had told us that Judge's wife moved into Miss Mary Lizzie Williamson's house and took care of Miss Mary Lizzie until she died. That's Miss Mary Lizzie's house right over there."

"It seems," said Cathy, "that someone told me that this was once just the Hosick Funeral Home."

"Yes," she answered, "My grandparents were here long ago. Granny and Pa lived in a house on this side of the street, down there toward the end of the parking lot, but after they died, it was torn down when my husband came into the business and we expanded the parking lot."

"Did the Stinsons have any children?" Cathy inquired.

"Lord, yes," came the reply, "It seems like my Uncle Eugene used to play with a boy who lived there. When I was a kid, we used to play hide and seek around those old houses over there until Mama forbade us to do so after my brother broke his arm when he fell off of the garden shed over at Miss Mary Lizzie's. I think Judge's widow still lived there long after all the kids were gone...I think."

Cathy could not understand the surge of emotions that were running through her right at this moment. She was just dying to go into Miss Mary Lizzie's back yard to see the remnants of the garden shed where Lynette used to meet K.C., where K.C. had lost his life, and where Baby had come to Lynette's rescue to help her conceal her crime.

"Here," Mrs. Tyler said taking a cell phone out of her coat pocket. "Let me call Mama and see if she remembers that woman's name."

Cathy thanked her and she and Gigi spoke quietly, gazing across the street to the old home place while Mrs. Tyler conducted her conversation. She imagined that Mrs. Tyler's mother had probably played on that front porch with some of the children named in the diary.

"Mama says that she thinks Mrs. Stinson's name is Lynette. And they had a grandson named Charles who used to play with my Uncle Eugene. She says that Mrs. Stinson will probably be able to tell you more about it."

"What?" Cathy gasped, "She's still alive?" She tried not to let her apprehension show, yet she was aquiver with excitement.

"Yes, Mama says that she thinks she's living over at the Shepherd-of-the-Hills in Chattanooga. She's way up in her nineties now."

Gigi stared at Cathy, and Cathy stared at Gigi, and then they both stared at Mrs. Tyler. Cathy gasped again, and Gigi, quick-witted and capable, said, "Oh, yes, I do believe I know her. She's one of my patients. I didn't know it was the same woman, Cat. I'll introduce you to her sometime." Mrs. Tyler believed Gigi's feigned truth.

Cathy's heart was racing. *How can this be? I've never seen her there!*

"Do you think anyone would care if we went over and looked at Lynette's house?" Cathy ventured.

"Yes," Gigi added, guessing, "She still talks about the beautiful garden she once had. We certainly would like to see where it was."

Cathy hastily agreed and was thankful for Gigi, a levelheaded girl who could think quickly on her feet. Mrs. Tyler pondered the request.

"I don't suppose it will do no harm," Mrs. Tyler said softly, as she walked Gigi and Cathy across the street. Stopping on the sidewalk, she pointed toward her right. "That's the old house place where Lynette and Judge lived, and this house right here is where she took care of Miss Mary Lizzie Williamson...up until she died, of course. I don't know if the house is locked or not."

"I'd love to see the inside," Cathy hinted.

"Well, I'd be mighty careful, if I was you," came the reply, "it's an old house and it's pretty run down."

"Oh, we will be, Mrs. Tyler, and thank you very much for your kindness," Cathy said, as she gently, and hurriedly, shook the woman's hand.

"Yes, thank you," Gigi added.

Before turning to go up the steps, they watched Mrs. Tyler make her way back across the street to the funeral home. The small town noises seemed to disappear as they walked up the steps. The screen door creaked as Cathy opened it, and the front door, with its antiquated knob, opened with very little effort.

"Well, "Gigi began as they stared around what was once the parlor, but was now a large, bare room with a high ceiling, "Mrs. Tyler is right. It's a rundown old house."

Cathy stared up at the faded walls whose pale paper, landscapes of castles and lakes in greens and browns, had bubbled and peeled in places, and had been entirely stripped in others. Her heart pounded as she recognized this wall paper from her dreams of the diary. These walls complemented the bare hardwood floors that were no longer magnificent, but scarred and buckled from too much moisture and no signs of life. She could see the parlor, once crowded with dim gilt Chinese cabinets that would make anyone curious to know what was in them, but were otherwise dispiriting as foggy antique mirrors, gloomy damasks and brocades, and lilies and orchids which Miss Mary Lizzie had never allowed to live out of doors.

When she saw the fireplace, a feeling stirred in her breast as she tried to imagine on the wooden mantel, two candelabra, like flat trees laden with prisms that refracted the sunlight into a spectrum of colors that played on the walls and objects about the room. What must it have been like for Lynette on the day that she had been sitting in front of a nice warm hearth in wait, while Baby's lifeblood seeped out into the icy waters of the Chickamauga?

How many times, Cathy wondered, had Lynette sat alone in the darkness hiding herself from the light? How many times had she sat in front of this fireplace seeming to read or knit, but actually pondering the illogical and irrational, her brain trying to rework the incorrect and make it correct?

As Cathy and Gigi strolled from room to room, she could only imagine to herself what she now knew had happened in them, but could not tell Gigi, as she felt that she would not understand the need. Her companion sensed that something was lacking in their conversation, and that her friend would explain when the time was right. The very life had been sucked out of the house, and now it was little more than a shell of its former self. There was no warmth in the kitchen, and if the aged walls could talk, Cathy somehow thought that they would refuse, in stony silence, to give up their secrets.

The two explorers cautiously climbed the worn wooden stairs and stood upon the broad landing for a moment. Cathy utilized a mental compass to determine the East Room from the West Room, as Lynette had called them, and opted to see Mable's room first. Her hands were moist and, to the touch, the doorknob felt inordinately cold. An eerie feeling passed as it dawned on her that she was standing in the same place where Mable and Miss Myrtle had stood so many times, and her hand was placed on exactly the same doorknob that Mable had turned so often without care. With a tightness in her chest, she turned the cold knob and entered the room.

She had no difficulty visualizing the room furnished with a large four-poster bed and canopy, and the accent chairs and draperies upholstered in crimson brocade. Outside the tall windows, oak branches tapped their twiggy fingers against the glass, propelled by air-eddies swirling haphazardly through the trees. The October morning dew had been evaporated by the burning sun, but despite the pleasant temperature in the shade of the oaks, the East Room could not be comforted, and it remained vacant and cold.

She and Gigi made their way back down the stairs and past what was once Miss Mary Lizzie's room, the room where she had died, and through the dingy green kitchen, and on to the back porch where Lynette would sneak away to check for a note from [C!] under the milk can. There was no milk can on the back porch now, and Cathy wondered where it had been.

She caught her breath when she looked out through the torn screen and saw what was left of Miss Mary Lizzie's garden shed. Gigi looked at her curiously.

"Let's go out there," Cathy said.

Miss Mary Lizzie's garden was a good forty-foot square, snug between four posts, two of which had held up an arbor for her grapevines at one end of the garden, and two of which had held three strands of clothesline at the other end. Unkempt and overgrown with weeds that choked the very beauty out of it, the garden reached out with ragged fingers, tendrils of creepers, to claim the clothesline posts and further on to what was left of the garden shed.

Cathy had no difficulty in sparking her imagination that this once-manicured plot of earth overflowed with all sorts of flowers and fragrance. She formulated the opinion that Miss Mary Lizzie had been orderly to a mathematical degree, and all of the beds had been bordered with mignonette and sweet alyssum, and within them the flowers had stood, pressing their glowing faces together in masses of riotous color—velvety red and pink roses, satin yellow California poppies, the heavenly blue of the cornflowers, crimson mallow, snow-white shining phlox, sweetbrier and carnations, and everywhere, the golden sparks of coreopsis.

Cathy's visionary talent enabled her to see splashes of burning scarlet, sheets of orange and lilac, and dashes of dazzling white. She saw the ferns, elephant ears, and their allies as simpler plants than those that had been planted as seeds, their histories showing her the alterations of generations, the former, larger and more abundant that had avoided extirpation. This garden had been considered, by far, the loveliest in all of Walker County.

"You mean that little shed? I don't know, Cat, it looks pretty grown up all around there. I'm afraid of snakes," Gigi responded.

"It'll be okay," she answered, snapping out of her daydream as she led the way across the back yard.

When she had made her way to the garden shed, she hesitated. Naked thorn bushes, inadequately held back by the remains of a trellis, encroached on the path to the shed. Being sere and leafless, they looked dead, but were viciously alive. Their bluish-red spikes, two to three inches long, tapered from quarter-inch bases to needle points. If Cathy or Gigi made a single incautious movement, they could fang flesh and into bone, as protectors of the gateway to the past, to matters that were no one's concern.

Gingerly edging their way past them, Cathy tested one of the points with her fingertip and was instantly rewarded with a gush of blood. Her finger felt as though it had been stung by a yellow jacket. Gigi handed her a tissue from her pocket and Cathy wrapped it around her finger and held it tightly until it had ceased to bleed.

Standing in front of the garden shed, Cathy noticed that creepers had overtaken the ramshackle structure, and the roof had fallen in. She peered into the open doorway, her eyes searching for the spot where Lynette had brought the shovel down on K.C. Fox and had ended his life. An old tarp covered most of what was left of the floor, and Cathy wanted to pull it back to see if she could find the spot where his life blood poured forth. Fearful of what she might find, she opted to leave the tarp alone, perhaps saving this wonderment for another outing.

Suddenly, Cathy turned to Gigi and said, "I wonder if this place is for sale!"

"You've got to be kidding," she laughed, heartily.

Still laughing, they made their way past the thorn bushes and back across the street to the funeral home parking lot. *I've just got to meet Lynette.*

Cathy had never been face to face with a murderer and the thought strangely intrigued her. When she and Gigi arrived back at the Hosick parking lot to get into their car, they saw Mrs. Hosick standing at the front door talking to two women. Cathy and Gigi waved to her as they passed, and she threw up her hand as she continued her conversation.

"Can we stop at the grocery on the way home?" Gigi asked.

"That sounds like a good idea," Cathy responded, "You making something special for dinner?"

"Yeah, Fred's been wanting to grill out. Want to join us?"

"Not tonight," Cathy smiled, "I'm making a sweet potato pie."

CHAPTER 26

Cathy and Gigi arrived back in Chattanooga later than she had expected. Her answering machine revealed two missed calls from Harry that were immediately returned while she was putting her dinner in the microwave. As they spoke, she spied a note from Heather on the kitchen table letting Cathy know that she and Michael were both out for the night and would not be home until late. Harry noticed disappointment in her voice.

"Okay," he said, "What is it?"

"Nothing, Sweetheart," came her reply, "Just missing you. Can't wait till you get home."

"Don't worry, Cat, I'll be back in a couple of days."

They spoke for a few more minutes, concluding with his promise to call her before he went to bed. The beeping of the microwave coincided with the ending of their conversation.

Gazing through the slider onto the deck, her attention was drawn to the setting sun. As the fireball sank lower and lower, it seemed to bleed from the sky, and the horizon was a broad luminous track of flame. Dazzling streaks of gold shot up through the firmament, meeting and penetrating hues of purple and blue. A glorious sunset, indeed. The slant of breeze had died away. A limitless calm seemed to benumb this space, to spread silence around this ritual when Nature readies herself for repose.

Twilight was short: the darkness gathered, studded with stars, and the cool of the evening expanded across the horizon. Time stood still as Cathy recorded the heavenly beauty of the sunset in her mind where tomorrow, she could recall it as an imaginary sunset on an imaginary landscape.

She made two sweet potato pies, one for Mr. Mack and one for Harry, and watched television in her recliner as they were baking. When she retired that evening, taking dinner on a tray, she felt strangely affected, and softened so that everything made her wish to cry. She couldn't explain it, which was just as well, for she had no one to whom she could explain.

Tomorrow, she and Gigi did not have to work, and had decided to stop by Shepherd-of-the-Hills in search of Lynette. Cathy slept very little that night, reading and rereading portions of the diary. Her dreams haunted her.

Lynette stood nervously in the kitchen lacing Judge's cocoa with poison and praying for strength, while Charles looked on with grave, curious eyes. Laughter drifted from the East Room as Mable and Hattie readied themselves for a night on the town. Soft, hushed tones dominated the parlor, where Ravanell and Ned sat conversing with William and Helen. Baby delivered milk and moonshine, while Mr. Mack and Thad did their time in jail. The garden shed held its secrets where Lynette lay in her lover's arms, enthralled with a great sensation, as if her flesh, her blood, and her bones were all melted together under her skin; the emptiness of reflection upon the decisive day that the dream of hope had become the nightmare of reality. Blood on the rocks, the cessation of light, the scarlet blot of sin.

Daybreak arrived before Cathy was prepared to meet it, her fitful sleep having refused her submersion into slumber. She found it difficult to collect her thoughts, let alone make sense out of them, as her nocturnal visitors were still milling about inside her head. The smell of fresh coffee filled her nostrils and her foresight to fill the coffee maker and set the timer allowed her to reap the benefit of "five more minutes" under the covers.

When she finally rose, she took her time readying herself. Unhurried fingers coiffed her short blond hairdo and she took her time drinking her coffee as she dressed for the day. Sporting blue jeans and a smart multicolored pullover sweater, Cathy sat in the kitchen smoking a cigarette. She wondered, when left alone in her later years, what Lynette had done to fill the ever-increasing void in her life.

When Gigi rang the doorbell around eightish, Cathy suddenly realized that she had promised to have breakfast ready when Gigi arrived. As she answered the door, Heather walked from the bathroom, across the hallway, to her bedroom. Smiling, Cathy called "good morning" to her daughter, as she opened the door and greeted her friend.

"I smell coffee, but I don't smell breakfast," Gigi began, "Did you just get up, girl?"

"No, I've been up awhile...time just got away from me."

"Well, move over, Gigi to the rescue!" With which Gigi turned to the kitchen, making a beeline for the fridge. "Bacon, eggs, toast?" she smiled, brightly.

"Works for me. Have at it," Cathy motioned, resuming her cigarette and coffee at the kitchen table.

As she watched Gigi preparing their meal, she marveled at how petite Gigi was, dressed in blue jeans and a long-sleeved tee shirt. They usually ordered the same thing when they dined together, however, Gigi's weight never seemed to change, while Cathy seemed to pack on the pounds.

Very little time had elapsed until they both sat at the table sampling Gigi's fare; after all, she was a good cook, indeed. Sensing her mood shifting, Cathy suddenly felt as she did before children, marriage, and even before love had come into her life; that her day was her own, and her hours were hers for inquisitive endeavors. She did not try to articulate this to Gigi, but she imagined that she, too, felt happy to be alive, preparing to go out with her friend, much as Mable and Hattie had done decades before.

Before long, the dishes were placed in the dishwasher and Cathy and Gigi, as well as the sweet potato pie, were out the door on their way to Shepherd-of-the-Hills. Over breakfast, they had formulated their plans as to how they would go about locating Lynette. When they had finally arrived at the nursing home, they stopped by their lockers to put on lab coats and identification badges which would allow them access to other floors of the facility. Cathy stealthily slipped the diary into her coat pocket.

Gigi chattered lightly as they made their way to the elevator and on to the second floor. The charge nurse, Hazel, greeted them cheerfully, "What have you got there, Cathy?"

"Oh," she laughed, "it's just a pie for Mr. Mack. Something to make him feel a little more at home."

"He'll like that, for sure, Cathy. He's one of Joan's

patients on day shift, but I can switch him over to you, if you want. I don't think Joan would mind. You and Wendy seem to get along quite well with him."

"That's fine with me," Cathy answered, and then ventured, "Hazel, a friend of mine told me about a woman who might be here," and then told her that she was looking for a woman from LaFayette named Lynette. While Cathy waited patiently and Gigi visited with some of the residents in the hall, Hazel searched the computer for anyone at the facility named Lynette, but to no avail. Perplexed, Cathy did not want her friend to sense her growing frustration and disappointment.

"This lady in Lafayette told me to come by here to see her and I said I would," Cathy said, skirting any suspicious issues.

"Well, let me keep looking ... wait, here's a Mrs. Lydia Peacock. She's on this floor."

"Thanks," Cathy said, smiling, "Gigi and I will just stroll around visiting a little bit and see if we can find her. Then, we'll have to go, so I won't be late." She feigned checking her watch for the time as if she were in a hurry.

The pair went to Mr. Mack's room first to deliver the pie and found him sitting up in bed watching television. His face lit up when Cathy walked through the door and set the pie on his table.

"My, my," he began, "Ain't this a su'prise." His gnarled hands fumbled with the remote to turn down the volume on the television.

"I just happened to be coming over today," Cathy said, "so I thought I'd bring you a treat."

"I'll get you a plate and a fork," Gigi offered, scurrying from the room.

Cathy took the opportunity to pick Mr. Mack's brain for more information. He told her he would help her anyway that he could.

"Do you remember when we were talking about Baby's sister, the one who was married to the hanging judge?"

Mr. Mack nodded, "Yes, I seen her here."

Her eyes widened considerably, so much that even Mr. Mack noticed it. She sat on the edge of his bed and whispered, "Where, Mr. Mack, where did you see her?"

"I don't recall," he said, looking at her intently, "but, I think I been here two, three days an' saw her in the hallway."

"Do you know where she is now?"

"No, ain't seen her since. Thought she looked familiar, but it might not been her. But, I rec'nized somethin' about her."

Gigi appeared in the doorway with plates and silverware. "Here, you go, Mr. Mack. You're in for a treat. Wendy's bringing you some juice."

His broad smile warmed Cathy's heart, and it made her feel good to think that she had eased someone's suffering. She cut the pie and heaped a generous portion onto his plate.

"You havin' some, ain't ya?"

"No, Mr. Mack, this is your pie. I've got another at home."

Wendy knocked as she entered the room and said, "Well, Mr. Mack, you didn't tell me you were having a party today."

Everyone laughed and the three workers chatted lightly among themselves until Mr. Mack said, "Ya'll go on so's I can watch my story." They laughed and said their good-byes before stepping out into the hall.

"Thanks," Wendy said, "You've made Mr. Mack's day. He's had a difficult time adjusting here." Cathy and Gigi quickly made their way down the hall to start looking for Lynette.

They stopped into Mrs. Lydia Peacock's room, and as she spoke of her home in Mississippi, Cathy cut their conversation short when she was sure that Mrs. Peacock was not Lynette. Cathy and Gigi trekked from floor to floor and ward to ward, chatting up the nurses and aides, trying to glean any information that they could. They checked for Lynettes or Mrs. Stinsons at each nurses' station until they had exhausted all of their efforts. Lynette Stinson was not there.

"Hey," Gigi stopped short, "What if she was here and has already died?"

"I don't know, Gigi, wouldn't we have heard about it?"

"Maybe, but, you know, you don't pay attention to every single one that passes, especially if they're not one of your patients."

A furrow in her brow, Cathy pondered that possibility as they returned to the second floor. They thanked their coworkers for their cooperation and bade them farewell until tomorrow.

"Well, I guess we wasted this day," Gigi, said as they walked toward the elevator.

As they passed Mrs. Shaw's door, the old woman called to them. Out of habit, Gigi stopped and stepped inside to check on her. Cathy waited patiently in the hall wondering where she would go from here.

As she leaned against the wall, she heard the voice of the charge nurse say to one of the aides, "Donna, go see if you can get Mrs. Oliver Graham something from the dining room. She's stopped eating again. I called the doctor and he's coming in tomorrow to check on her."

Cathy froze. *Mrs. Oliver Graham? From the diary? Lee Graham is here?* She stepped over to the nurses' station, "Hazel, are you talking about our Mrs. Graham?"

"Yes," she answered, "Why?"

"I think she might be a friend of the woman I've been trying to locate. Is her first name Lee?

"Let me check, Cathy," Hazel said, "No, it doesn't say Lee. She listed as Cora L. Graham."

"Maybe, the L stands for Lee," Cathy offered.

"No," Donna broke in, overhearing their conversation. "Her name's not Lee. She's Miss Lynn."

"Cathy, that could be your Lynette," Hazel said, decisively.

"Where is she now?" Cathy asked.

"She's still in 17," Donna said, "C'mon, I'll take you to see her. I'm going there right now to see what she wants to eat."

"Hazel, if Gigi comes looking for me, tell her I'll be right back," Cathy said, following Donna down the hall to the room on the right, Room 17. She could feel the tension of the anticipation and the excitement of discovery as she stopped outside Miss Lynn's door.

Donna knocked softly as she gently pushed the door open. "Miss Lynn? It's me, Donna, I came to see if I could get you to eat something for me. Doctor says you gotta eat. You gotta keep up your strength."

Receiving no reply, Donna turned to Cathy, "Go on ahead and talk to her while I run down to the dining room and get her a little ice cream or something, maybe one of her shakes she likes to drink." With that said, Donna excused herself.

"Okay, I'll be right here," Cathy said.

Even though the room was dark when she entered, the figure of an old woman sitting up in bed was clearly visible. Her heart quickened and she felt her pulse beating as she gazed upon this woman, Lynette, whom she had come to know so well. Had she not been made privy to the incidents of murder, Cathy would never have guessed that this frail creature could have ever been mixed up in such matters.

"Ms. Graham? Are you Lynette Graham?" Cathy ventured.

"Who are you?" the weak voice crackled.

"It's me, Cathy, Ms. Graham," she said, making her way to the woman's bedside.

"Come in, dear," she answered weakly, "I can't see you."

"Do you want me to turn on the light?"

"If you please," Lynette formed her words, carefully. Cathy found her to be polite and, in every respect, a southern lady.

Cathy turned on the lamp and sat in a chair next to Mrs. Graham's bed, trying to relate this nonagenarian to the vision of the young Lynette that she held in her mind, but the elder's aging eyes would not reveal the past. Her eyes seemed different, deeply set, not as though she were wincing at anything, but as though they had retreated from a sight that she had found to be disagreeable. Even though they were not sad eyes, or weary eyes, for that matter, Cathy assumed that they were eyes that would never again widen with surprise. However, she found that, as circumstances would have it, she was wrong.

As she looked at the elderly woman, Cathy could see that she was not well, her translucent sallow skin revealing her unhealthy color. It was equally evident that Lynette did not recognize Cathy, for she smiled a small forced, timid smile. Cathy felt a tightness in her chest and her mind was flooded with a million questions to ask, but she didn't know where to begin. Not particularly gifted with character analysis, she was unable to define the complex series of events that had drawn them together, but a dormant instinct told her that this interlude was more than functional; it was organic and structural, as the Cosmos, and certainly not accidental.

She looked around the darkened room, drinking in the comfortable feel of it. Lynette must admire flowers and birds, Cathy thought, as she noticed pictures and figurines placed around the room, hidden in the shadows. It had never occurred to her that perpetrators of murder could be culturally drawn. Amid the pictures and figurines, she spied a small silver frame sitting on a low antique end table beside her. The woman in the photograph appeared to be somewhat manly, yet her broad smile exuded an air of motherliness about her. *Baby!*

She decided to take out the diary to see if there were any reaction from Mrs. Graham. As Cathy pulled it from her pocket, she could tell that Lynette recognized it immediately. A look of shock, maybe horror, froze on the old woman's face, and she looked as though she'd just been punched. Tears welled up in the old woman's eyes, and silently ran down her cheeks. She was the one.

After a moment, she stammered, "Where...

where...," her wet lips were quivering, but the words were never uttered. Cathy hurriedly put the diary back in her pocket as Donna came into the room, followed by Gigi.

Lynette's tall thin frame, to which her cotton gown hung loosely, was palpitating, shaking with convulsions. She expelled a loud moan as her sorrow was overtaking her.

"You okay, Ms. Graham?" the aide asked, rushing from the door.

Mrs. Graham expelled another loud moan as Gigi took her hand. Her puzzled look made Cathy uneasy. They could see her bony ankles and withered limbs covered with thick blue stockings, shaking horribly. Cathy fixated on the hard, even colors of the counterpane between Lynette's crooked fingers, receiving indifferently, repeated clawing as, unconsciously, Lynette dug into the mattress as if to make a grave in which to hide herself.

After a few moments, the convulsions ceased, and Lynette breathed heavily through her parched lips. As Gigi patted Miss Lynn's hand, Donna gave her a sip of water which she drank greedily.

"What happened?" the aide asked, looking over at Cathy, who was visibly shaken.

"I-I don't know," Cathy stammered, crossing her fingers behind her back. She knew in an instant that she had frightened the old woman out of her senses.

"Don't you scare me like that, Miss Lynn. You feeling better now?"

Lynette shook her head affirmatively, a solitary tear creating a rivulet traversing a wrinkle in her face. Her vacant stare could not be broken, not even by her incessant mumbling, and her countenance remained unchanged. Her long bony hands continued to tremble.

"I don't think Ms. Graham is up to company right now."

"Oh, I understand," Cathy said, and she stood up and went to the bedside and put her arms around Mrs. Graham. "I'll come back to see you later, after you've had time to rest." She leaned closer to hug Lynette and whispered in her ear, "Don't worry. Your secret's safe with me. I'll see to it that you take it to the grave."

"Bless you, child," Mrs. Graham mumbled feebly, "Bless you...bless you ...."

Lynette lay still, one hand clutching the edge of the patchwork quilt that covered her, and the other hand held to her chest. She felt as though the world had imploded upon her, leaving her no recourse.

That being stated, Cathy turned and left the room so quickly that not even Gigi could make out her expression. It would have been difficult, in any event, as her face was so withholding. Cathy was sorry now that she had given herself the satisfaction of surprise without fully revealing her intention to Lynette. To her, it was merely a puzzle to be solved, an excursion to pass away the hours; but, to Lynette, it was the difference between living and dying, facing another person with what was surely meant to be between her and God. It was hard to know how people of that sort would respond to what certainly seemed to be an act of retributive justice, possibly of a harsh appearance to those who had no knowledge of the diary. Harsh or not, it was done.

Chapter 27

Gigi was not waiting for Cathy when she pulled into her parking space the next morning. She did not think much of it at the time, as Gigi had been late for work on occasion. Cathy felt a presentiment of impending discourse, but not so much that she knew exactly what it could be, as she rode the elevator to the second floor. As she exited, she was aware of an unusual silence at the nurses' station.

"What's going on?" Cathy asked, nonchalantly, holding her breath, bracing for bad news. "Is Gigi okay?"

"Gigi's fine. Her car wouldn't start and Fred's bringing her to work," Hazel said.

"Then," Cathy asked again, "What's going on?"

"Well, it's Mrs. Graham...."

"Mrs. Graham? I'll go see her."

"Cathy, wait...Cathy," she hesitated, "Mrs. Graham coded this morning. She's gone."

An errant frenzy seized her, having nothing to do with hope or success, and running at breakneck speed to Lynette's room, Cathy's heart was racing and her insides seemed gelatinous. *Oh, God! Oh, God!*

Lynette's bed was empty; the body removed. The harsh overhead lights illuminated the entire vastness of Lynette's last abode. The stark expanse revealed that the walls were actually pale green, and Cathy winced at the thought that she had never noticed that before.

She began an immediate search of the room and the bath, after noticing two boxes next to the wall into which the aides had placed the remains of Lynette's belongings. Into one box, they had emptied the medicine cabinet of all that was in any way personal to Lynette, including the standard contents: iodine, adhesive tape, a bottle of aspirin, a box of bicarbonate of soda. They had scoured the room and into the other box put all that they had found: bottles, note paper, old letters, hair pins, lotion bottles, combs and brushes, and the remains of her clothing.

She then espied a small basket where they had placed odds and ends, a scrapbook, the silver frames that held the pictures of her family, and one that she now knew had to be Baby. Resting on top of the contents was a photograph album, but somehow, Cathy's curiosity could not be aroused. All too soon, the room had been made complete. It was restored, taken from Lynette, for the next elderly resident whose mind or body would refuse to cooperate with their children, necessitating their incarceration, as it were, in what they knew would be their last home on Earth.

Suddenly with sadness, Cathy thought, "And whosever shall not receive you, nor hear you, when you depart thence, shake off the dust under your feet for a testimony against them."

Was that a verse from the Bible? She tried hard to recall, but her mind was foggy. The aides had shaken the dust off of Lynette's room, a testimony against her.

Cathy sat down on the edge of Lynette's bed that had

been stripped down to the plastic mattress cover. For a long time she sat, her shoulders bowed, and her hands listless on her knees. With hot cheeks, she tried to recall what she had said to Lynette. She looked up through glistening eyes and saw Gigi standing in the doorway. A hard knot in her throat prevented her from speaking, and she felt sick to her stomach.

"Take your time, Cat," Gigi offered, "I'll cover for you until you get on the floor, okay?"

Cathy shook her head in jerking motions. *She's dead because of me...I killed her...I am responsible.* She could not articulate these thoughts to Gigi, but felt that she already seemed to know.

"It's not your fault, Cat. It was her time to go," Gigi proffered, unaware of the conversation in Cathy's head.

Cathy felt the sting of hot, silent tears as Gigi turned and walked down the hallway to make their rounds. Her nose had begun to run and her eyes burned, but she found that Lynette's tissues had already been packed into one of the boxes, so she sniffed repeatedly, blotting her nose with her sleeve. Even though her face was bathed in tears, it took on a radiance of some mysterious, hidden triumph, and now she wondered what had spurred her need to know—her need to be right.

Normally, the room temperature was on the cool side, but today seemed warm and oppressive. Still sitting on the side of Lynette's bed, Cathy closed her eyes, breathed deeply, and tried to relax, but it was not easy, as she felt that the inertia of the air had deepened and could not be shifted. She found herself reliving the scenario with Lynette, and the many sentiments that she could have said, *should have said,* until the thoughts became blurred and she could not separate them. She thought nothing clearly, until a dawning of what Lynette must have felt began to weigh heavily upon her: the searing of humiliation and the consciousness of being cheated, derided, and alone.

Now, Cathy could only think of how throughout her life. Lynette had struggled futilely among the nettles of despair, flung into circumstances that thrust her into definitive ruin, and now she had taken the final step. Like someone's breath on a mirror, everything that had meant anything to her, her home and her family, had disappeared without her ever knowing why.

Cathy, herself, felt as though a thousand arrows of regret and shame were quivering in her own heart; the guilt of having, too, committed a crime and shielding her own foolish actions. *Oh! Why did I have to show that diary to Lynette!* If her own misdeed were ever to come to light, she, too, could possibly be discharged from her job or could legally be prosecuted. She would lose caste among her peers, and even though some would still tolerate her, her words would no longer carry any weight and she would never again be taken seriously.

"I'm sorry to disturb you, Miss Cathy," said an aide from the open doorway, "but, the family is coming today to collect Miss Lynn's things. Should I leave them in here?"

Cathy wasn't so much concerned with the girl's indecision as she was with the lack of self-reliance it indicated. Still, her light southern lilt was soothing to the tattered edges of Cathy's spirit, and she momentarily felt ashamed for being judgmental.

She opened her eyes and wiped her face with her hands. The hard knot in her throat had subsided to a cool lump, and her temples had begun to throb.

Strangely, her attention was drawn to a whatnot, where a miniature castle made of squares of perforated cardboard worked into a single zephyr and caught together at the angles, was dangling from a knob on the top shelf.

"I know it's hard when you get attached to your patients," the aide comforted, realizing that she had disturbed Cathy in a vulnerable moment, and instinctively stepped back. There was something in this shrinking movement that touched Cathy, however, she could not help but wonder how the castle was made and she could not focus. Her sorrow and curiosity were confused and distorted, bumping into each other inside her head, each vying for her attention.

Shaking her head silently, Cathy did not divulge that she had barely known Lynette, and grimly thought of Lynette crying at Judge's grave, and her neighbors proffering consolation, not knowing that her sorrow was not that of a dutiful widow. After the aide had left the doorway, Cathy quickly grabbed up the photograph album and held it against her and headed for the locker room. *I'm just going to borrow this for a while,* she rationalized.

The remnants of Lynette dominated her thoughts for the rest of the day, and as she looked out the window, she saw threatening clouds, distended with thunder lying supine in the sky, awaiting a gestating storm. When the rain set in, the world was, indeed, depressing. Harry called and said that he had been dispatched to make another run to New York and would be gone another four days, and that made Cathy's world desolate and disparaging, as angry clouds collided overhead. She could not wait for him to get back home so she could unburden herself, and tell him all that had happened.

This had not been a passive day, and its demands had taken their toll on her. By the end of her shift, the storm had finally passed the zenith; its spent thunder, trundling off to the east, and the wind had steadied under its burden of rain. Driving home was particularly difficult as a thick fog had set in and unrolled its billowy, white blanket, enveloping her and hiding her in the darkness.

Only white was visible when she turned on her high beams, so she had to settle for being barely able to see beyond the yellow glow of the low beams, parenthesized by droplets of water that were shiny black pearls on her windshield. Streetlights appeared to be large fuzzy balls of light suspended on an invisible thread sewn through the vaporous cotton of the night, and tail lights flashed out warnings of danger throughout the whiteness. Patience and diligence brought her home safely, but emotionally and physically drained of energy.

Michael and Heather were already home and in for the night, she hoped. Perhaps, she'd shower and go to bed early, take dinner on a tray, and read. There was really no one to consider now, save herself.

She lay on her bed and pondered the events of the day, still stunned at all that had transpired so rapidly. The last thing that she had wanted to do was to cause another person's death, or at the very least, hasten it. Alone in her room, Cathy sighed as she sat cross-legged on her bed, nibbling on the meager portions from the tray, listening to the rain that had started pelting against the windowpane.

Shortly before midnight, Cathy called Gigi, and the two decided to go to the Tyler-Hosick Funeral Home tomorrow evening for the visitation. Gigi informed her that the funeral was set for Wednesday, the day after, and she didn't really want to go, but Cathy felt that it was now her duty, and begged Gigi to go with her.

Overwhelming fatigue gripped Cathy when she talked to Harry, who sensed that something was dreadfully wrong. She tried to explain some of it, and Harry tried to listen, but she could not verbalize it, not right now. They kissed good night over the phone, again, and Cathy told him that when he got home, she would sit down and explain everything to him.

With renewed interest, despite her fatigue and a pain in her head, Cathy retrieved the photograph album and settled back to examine its contents. *It would be nice to be able to put a face to the name,* she mused, as she carefully open its worn leather cover.

On the first page, in all of its original white, gleaming splendor, was Lynette's house, or when this picture was taken, Miss Mary Lizzie's. A short frail little old lady with stooped shoulders covered by a white shawl, attempted to stand regally erect, her hands clasped before her. The town matriarch's misty eyes, Cathy surmised to be blue, shone brightly and appreciative, and twinkled from an etching of wrinkles. Atop her queenly head was a tight crown of snowy hair from which cascaded a long silver braid. The hem of her long black dress looked as though it were suspended above her high-topped shoes, and at her throat was a high white collar, restrained by a distinctive Cameo brooch. Cathy's breath quickened as she realized that this was Miss Mary Lizzie.

Gingerly, she turned the large black page, exercising great care, lest any of the pages had stuck together. Dr. Arthur Warrenfells, who knew that most people were left without resources during and after the Great Depression, only charged twenty-five dollars to deliver a baby, and the ones who couldn't pay cash, paid him with chickens, squirrels, vegetables, and pecans. He had brought most of Walker County's citizens into the world, and was the one who had pronounced a good many as having departed at their journeys' ends. Tall, gray-haired and distinguished, he would not abide gossip, and held his patients' ailments, troubles, and crises in strictest regard and confidence; the most respected man in the county.

Cathy found a snapshot of an Orenduff Dairy milk truck, and standing beside it, wearing a work shirt, trousers, and dark brogans, was robust Baby, the keeper of all secrets and the best friend that Lynette could have ever had in this world. A woman of masculine proportions, towering, barrel-chested, large-limbed Baby wore her light-colored hair short, in a page-boy style. Her face shone forth an unmistakable motherliness, as if the world at large were her family, and it had been her business to see that all were generously provided for, along the most pleasingly possible lines for all concerned.

Cathy shuddered to think that the truck by which Baby stood was the same one that she could not control on the ice, resulting in her untimely death at the age of twenty-five. She imagined that as Baby lay dying on the bank of the Chickamauga in the dead of winter, she could hear the babbling of the water over rocks, the silence of the bleak woodland, and the beat of angels' wings in the heartless voice of the cold, lonely wind.

Aunt Ellen's wide mouth was framed with dark lipstick, at times drawn outside the contours, proudly displaying her new dentures when she smiled. Her light orchid face wrinkled and puckered like a tomato beneath her dark hair, throughout which ran streaks of gray. She wore a gabardine suit tailored to her embonpoint, and on her head sat an odd, shapeless hat that tilted to one side. Cathy stared at the face of Papa's baby sister, who was Baby's namesake, and whom Lynette had taken to her appointments with Dr. Winslow, and had waited on the bus with her through the ordeal of procuring new dentures.

Cathy read notations on small pieces of paper taped beneath the photographs. Aggravation set in when she found pictures that had none, and she could not identify as people mentioned in the diary, but she knew they were there. She just didn't know where.

Judge Charles Stinson was a serious young man who had turned into a serious old man, Cathy ascertained. He appeared to have lived absorbed in his own profession, and when he was not contemptuous, he was indifferent to the world. If he had a purely human emotion, it was pride, as Lynette had said, and he never had been so great a fool as to genuinely care for any human creature. He endured his family members and fellow beings, and was just to them, or so he said. But, he never knew a man, woman, or child who could not be bought and sold like a bale of cotton.

Next to Judge's picture, Cathy found his obituary, and was curious as she smoothed out the folded column, yellowed and brittle with age, that had been cut from the weekly paper. She read, silently, the last account of his remembrance.

Funeral Saturday Afternoon for Judge Stinson

Was Superior Court Judge of Walker County for Twenty-Two Years—Loveable Character—Large Crowd Attended Funeral Rites

Judge Charles Braxton Stinson, 67, died early Thursday at his home on Mulberry Street, after an illness of several months.

The death of Judge Stinson removes from LaFayette and Walker County one of the best known and most highly esteemed citizens. He served as Superior Court Judge of Walker County from 1914 until 1935, when he retired from office due to ill health. During his long career as a public official, he served the public in a highly efficient manner, evidenced by his reelection each successive term.

The kindness of his spirit, his broad charity, unassuming manner, and his sympathies for all mankind, were qualities that coordinated in his life and in his personality and were responsible for his universal popularity, as a man and public official. Devoted to his family and friends; loyal to his church; a faithful and competent public servant, his demise is deeply deplored.

Judge Stinson was twice married. His first wife was Miss Amelia Pennington of East Armuchee Valley, who died in 1919, and he was also preceded in death by his eldest daughter, Evelyn Rose Chambers (Hudson), who died in 1931. His second wife by whom he is survived, was formerly Miss Cora Lynette Orenduff, of Rock Spring.

He is survived by two daughters, Miss Mable Charlene Stinson, of the residence, and Mrs. Sara Jane Baker (Edwin), of Chattanooga, Tennessee; and also, two grandchildren, Miss Karen Ravanell Stinson (Mable), and Master Charles Randall Chambers (Evelyn), both of the residence.

Funeral services were held Saturday afternoon from the First Baptist Church, of which he was a faithful member, with his pastor, Rev. L.L. Story officiating, assisted by Rev. James Willard Cash. Interment was in the Garden of Light Cemetery, with Hosick Funeral Home in charge. Pallbearers were Edwin Baker, Ned Potts, Tom Shields, Oliver Graham, Tommy Quinlan, and William Derryberry.

The church was filled with sorrowing friends and relatives, and many beautiful floral tributes were sent as tokens of the esteem in which he was held.

Cathy weighed the information in the obituary against what she knew privately about him and decided that the glowing testament was the way that his family had wanted him to be remembered. That the man had been intellectually superior, and intensely difficult to abide, must have been apparent to the most superficial observers, yet the minions tolerated his abuse and touted his generosity. Playground equipment and new pews for the church could soften the truth, which would have been unnecessarily forthright and would have been a poor substitute for comfort during his family's time of grief. Doubting that his distasteful demeanor had been simulated by those nearest to him, Cathy carefully folded the yellowed strip and placed it as she had found it, before turning the page.

Evelyn, Judge's deceased eldest daughter, had married a good-for-nothing scalawag, Hudson Chambers, who had swept her away to Nashville and had not taken care of her as he had promised Judge. She was so ill-treated that he allowed her no proper medical care, so much that within seven years of their marriage, she had succumbed to a quiescent tumor—leaving behind one child whom she had named after her father.

Sara, the youngest Stinson daughter, was pictured wearing a low-necked evening dress, with a piece of black velvet tied in a bow around her throat, and a grandiose ornament of jewels adorned her upswept coiffure. Cathy had pictured her as being rugged and businesslike, but the photograph, taken from a side view, gave Sara a smoothed-out expression, not particularly life-like, but exceptionally beautiful.

Charles's photograph portrayed a silent child, with mild, wide brown eyes, and straight, silken brown hair parted over his candid forehead. Cathy recognized his eyes from his mother's photograph, and felt sorrow that Evelyn had not lived to see how handsome her young man had grown. Such a loving and giving boy, Lynette had praised him, and had seen to it that he had had his own bicycle to go riding with Walter Cobb.

Lynette was a lovely woman, fair of face. No one, except Baby, knew this woman who had found it hard to endure the tension between need and satisfaction; this woman who, in her waning years, knew the hell of being left with herself, no one in whom she could confide. Time and space might have distanced her from the scenes of murder, but they traveled with her in her heart, proving that the self one has to live with can be one's greatest punishment. Despite employing self-restraint, effort, and discipline to remain true to her God and her religion, want and need had propelled her to seek out and experience what she thought to be true love, leaving her with emptiness; imprisoned and sentenced by the court of her own conscience.

Her marriage to Judge had been a living martyrdom, yet still she had robbed her soul of honor and fidelity. Lynette had convinced herself that in its inception, their love had been personal, when in cold hard truth, it was social, and she had served as little more than a maid or housekeeper, who just happened to share his bed, truckling to his every whim.

Mable's world was totally different from Lynette's, as Mable was free. Every flash of a laugh or smile was a thorn to Lynette, and every spark of happiness a reproach; *how envy marked its victim.* Judge, truculent, oppressive, and unchangeable as the dog days of summer, had told her that she, too, had been any and one of the nameless and faceless, whom had been bought and sold like a bale of cotton. Condemned by the darkness in her heart, her sorrow was deep and her soul was devoid of joy.

Ravanell was a mere girl, golden-haired with pearly white teeth. A stunning high school senior, it was clear to Cathy that she had inherited her mother's beauty and fair complexion. However, Ravenell's eyes were distinct and familiar, yet Cathy could not remember where she had seen them before. Her stature seemed to be petite and gangly, and Cathy could tell by her effeminate stance that the girl didn't have a tomboyish bone in her body. In many ways, Ravanell reminded Cathy of Heather, but despite her teenage appearance, her eyes foretold that she had matured beyond her years.

Cathy carefully turned the black pages of the album, pausing to read the little notations. "Mable and Hattie, 1936" she read under a small rectangular photo. Blond-haired Mable, who had never grown up, was still a girl in her thirties, embracing life and relishing the good times that were offered her, treating her own daughter more like a sister instead of her own child.

Dark-haired Hattie was donned in a smart, stylish outfit that complemented her slim figure, and she and Mable were portrayed standing in front of the auto that Dr. Winslow had bought for her and that had ultimately become her death trap. Poor Hattie, who had never set out to be seductive, was born to circumstances that were such that Lynette could not compete with her for K.C.'s favor. However, as pictured, their sparkling smiles and fresh, youthful appearance hid any signs that the two were more than schoolgirls out to frolic.

They lived on a merry-go-round of happiness, always purchasing expensive garments, jewelry, furs, and many fine things with money they never earned, and enjoying every bit of it; hosting dinners and teas and parties, quite the heiresses, in their opinions, and thought the world a very pleasant place in which to live. The more money that men spent on them, the nicer they could be. The attention they lavished was merely superficial, but still the suitors lined up to be with them. Their lifestyles and lives seemed to be pristine and free of any depression-era anxieties that had plagued most of their neighbors.

Cathy thumbed through the pages meeting Ravanell and Ned, and Emily and Tommy and Little Joe, together for a family snapshot, standing in front of Quinlan's Barber Shop, passed down to Tommy from his father; and Helen and William on their wedding day; Oliver and Lee Graham and their son, Perry, relaxing on the airy front porch of their Maple Street home; and Georgia Mae and Edsel Turner and Baby Florene, smiling for the camera outside the Baptist church after Easter Sunday services; and Charles and Walter Cobb, the day they had ridden their bicycles to Rock Spring and back; and Miss Mary Lizzie, Mrs. Hosick, and Lynette drinking lemonade one hot afternoon on the front porch of their home on Mulberry Street.

One photograph portrayed Mable, dressed in a pastel taffeta evening gown, adorned with jewelry, standing in front of the moon-blued columns of the Grammar School, no doubt the night she had attended the

Roosevelt Ball. Next to it, another photograph of Mable and Ravanell, again, more like sisters than mother and daughter.

Another photograph that caught her attention was of a man and a woman and their three children. The man, lean and muscular, whose dark eyes exuded an air of mystery, seemed confident and capable. His wife, though still a young woman, had not aged as gracefully as her husband, but was not homely, just mature and matronly. She was the one who held her family together, and portrayed this in the picture by huddling her three children around her, as a mother hen would harbor her chicks. Cathy read the small, yellowed strip of paper taped below the picture, "K.C. and Lucile, Kerry, Jimmy, and Seab. *It's nice to put a face to the name.*

Realizing that this was a photo of K.C. Fox, Cathy began to understand what Lynette had seen in him. He was, indeed, a handsome man, and evidently had utilized this asset to have his way with women, discarding his past with heartless superiority, she assumed. Longing for the comfort of a family, and being opposed by the need for human fulfillment, Lynette and Lucile had each, in their own ways, compromised themselves by their involvement with him in order to secure their futures; each unaware of his wanton philandering, and each losing to the fateful forces of the Cosmos.

Chapter 28

Many had gathered at the Tyler-Hosick Funeral Home to see Lynette one last time. Cathy did not know any of the people there and felt oddly out of place. Yet, she found it strange that she should know Lynette better than anyone in attendance. Many visitors stood in line to view Lynette as she lay in her casket, while others talked quietly in groups, catching up on old times, as though Lynette's passing were an ordinary happening. A person's death only happens once, Cathy thought, and it should be special.

When she and Gigi stopped to sign the guest book, her eyes scanned the page for the name "Mary Elizabeth," but she did not find it. They made their way to the line for viewing, and while they waited, Mrs. Tyler approached and welcomed them. Her brunette head bobbed as she waddled toward them, and her warm smile was a comfort to Cathy.

"I want you to meet someone," she began, and the three left the viewing line.

"Marty," she placed her hand on a man's arm and he turned around. "Marty, I want you to meet some of your mama's friends."

"Hello," he said, shaking Cathy's hand, "I'm Martin Stinson."

Mrs. Tyler's soothing southern voice continued, "Marty is Lynette's son. Marty, I want you to meet Cathy and Gigi. They work at Shepherd-of-the-Hills and helped take care of your mama until she passed."

Cathy could not believe her eyes. *Lynette did not have a girl! She'd had a boy!* The thought had never occurred to her, and she was quite taken aback. Martin Clyde Stinson stood before her, older and distinguished, handsome, in fact, and she did not know what to make of it. She found a familiarity about him, for she was not looking into Lynette's eyes. Her head was reeling and she had so many questions welling up inside of her, pushing to be asked and answered, but her shock was apparent, as she stood agape.

"I'm so grateful to you for taking care of Mama," Martin Stinson began, as he extended his large hand to Gigi, "She was so feeble her last days."

"We were glad to do it, Mr. Stinson. We all loved Miss Lynn," Gigi responded, shaking his hand immediately when she realized that Cathy, speechless, could only stare into his dark, distinctive eyes. The point of Gigi's elbow in her ribs returned her faculties.

Cathy regained her composure and stammered, "I-I think one of Miss Lynn's photo albums was left behind. I can bring it tomorrow...when we come for the funeral."

"That would be just fine," he replied, softly.

"Maybe," Cathy continued, "after the funeral...maybe, we could stop and have a cup of coffee...and talk...maybe."

He shook his head and smiled a comforting smile, "That would be nice. Charles is going to be here tomorrow and I haven't seen him in a while. He loved Mama dearly. Maybe, he could join us?"

Gigi's dark eyes grew wide in bewilderment when she saw Cathy's jaw drop. "Sure, sure," Cathy stammered for words, "We'd love to meet him, wouldn't we, Gigi?"

"Yes, yes. Is Charles your brother?"

"No, no, Charles is my nephew, even though he's twelve years older than me. He's the son of my sister from Daddy's first marriage."

This development was mind-boggling, and Cathy wondered what other surprises were in store. The thought of Charles Chambers being alive had never even occurred to her. Excitement churned inside her, instantly accompanied by shame. She had not meant to be the firebrand that had sent Lynette to her demise, and she felt wickedness at her position to exploit the situation to fulfill her frivolous need to satisfy the diary's unanswered questions.

* * *

Upon returning home, Cathy prepared her dinner, putting the tray on her nightstand instead of the computer table. Beyond that, the next few hours were not altogether clear to her, but at some point, she had eaten. She had tried to watch television, but had fallen into a light slumber. Awakening, her body felt sticky and uncomfortable, so she decided to undress. She was hot and sweating, so she quickly showered before donning fresh night clothes and her bedroom slippers.

Cathy opened her bedroom door and peered out into the deserted hallway. All was quiet, so she carefully closed the door and locked it with a sense of satisfaction and relief. She did not want her nocturnal visitors to find their way into her bedroom tonight.

Lying in bed later that night, Cathy snuggled under the covers missing Harry. Her children were home and already in bed, yet Cathy was still robbed of sleep. As she thought about her day, and her life, she felt the sensations of frustration and anger welling within her. She could find no peace or rest. This autumn had begun with such promise and exhilaration and now the days had become distorted and tangled, just as the thoughts streaming through her head. She stared at the ceiling, noticing a small cobweb in a far corner, and made a mental note to sweep it away in the morning.

The diary beckoned her once more from the nightstand, but she did not give in to it; not tonight. It was just a book, or so she thought. She knew that the people in the diary were not imaginary, yet their reality had not sunk in until the death of Lynette. Even though she had not developed the intent, Lynette's demise was at her hands and on her heart.

Avoiding scathing accountability in this world, Cathy knew that she would have to face it in the next, and the prospect worried her. Her karmic debt would take its place with the rest of her baggage and all of what she would have to face one day. Now, Lynette was facing her own karmic debt, and Cathy wondered how she would be required to pay it. Each night from here on out, if she could sleep, she would fall asleep begging forgiveness.

The figures continued to haunt her dreams. As deeply rooted as her fear was, this situation was totally out of control, and there was no way to stop these people from coming to her. They milled about inside her head, speaking, living, loving, and dying, just as they had done in 1938. The invaders were a composite of the whole town, and in her dreams, Cathy recognized even the ones she did not know. She tried to shut her eyes and clear her mind, but still they managed to get in.

* * *

The service the following afternoon was lovely. *Such a sweet funeral, as Lynette would've said. Many wonderful friends and family members were in attendance.* Cathy imagined what Lynette would have written in her diary.

Cathy and Gigi sat in the back of the chapel observing the small, subdued group of people who had gathered to bid Lynette adieu. A solemn occasion, it was more melancholy than it was devastating, as the mourners believed that Lynette's time had come. Charles, grateful to Lynette for his boyhood, gave the eulogy, reading one of her favorite poems, "The Earth Is No More My Home," by Gertrude Henderson Swain.

Charles was a short, sturdy-looking man with a soft gray beard, and kind, quiet, nearsighted eyes, which his round, gold wire-rimmed spectacles magnified into lambent moons. There was no weakness in his face; but, there was patience in every line he spoke.

"The Earth is no more my home," his voice projected clearly and concisely as he looked at the small gathering. As Charles spoke and Cathy listened, she could not help but to imagine Lynette, sitting in her parlor in front of the fireplace, pondering her own demise, wondering what she could do to make amends for the harm she had done; atonement for the havoc she had wreaked, seeking a way out when there was none. Now, she was going back to the Earth and would become an integral cog in Nature's life cycle, in the grand design of Life, and in death, perpetuating Nature's new green. Charles continued:

"When I am dead and gray,
I'll no longer be aware of rain,
Or spring, or new mown hay.
My eyes won't see; my ears won't hear;
My body will not feel the tears
Of people whom I love.
But, separately, I nothing know
From my repose below.
The strange and earthly beauty's gone
For now my time to count has come
And I will pay the debt I owe
In service to the fields and trees,
And help the flowers grow,
That I might rise above.

Here, the sadness was apparent in Charles's voice and shone through his eyes, and he paused briefly to wipe them. Then, he culminated, "I loved Lynette, and she owes nothing. Her debt here on Earth is paid in full."

Now, Cathy was wondering if Charles had any knowledge of the diary...or about what Lynette had done. Maybe she had confided in him...or maybe he had secretly watched her and made the decision not to betray the one person who truly loved him.

Cathy felt a hard lump welling in her throat, and this part of the service gave her pause to stop and think. She likened Lynette to a drop of water in a gutter, dirty and soiled, finding no favor, when suddenly it is met by a friendly sun, kissed and uplifted to the heavens. By grace and forgiveness, this small drop of water had been transformed into a perfect snowflake resting on a mountain top. She must be in Shangri La, she thought, in reference to the mystical place in the Himalayas where, it is believed, the soul goes to rest immediately following death.

As the final viewing began, Cathy sat quietly taking in the soft, precise appearance of the funeral home, and the unmistakable fragrance of funeral flowers filled her nostrils. The music filled her with sadness as she and Gigi brought up the end of the line for the final viewing. Cathy stared down at the person whose face, though wonderfully peaceful, showed that she had been no stranger to sorrow, and whose heart held secret upon secret. Wearily, Lynette had known the education of Life, truly; the multiplication table of anxieties and sorrows, the subtraction table of loss, the division table of responsibility. But, more importantly, she had known the addition table of hope.

Lynette is free now. Such a sweet funeral, just what Lynette would've said, Cathy thought as she sat down next to Gigi, who sat silently chewing a stick of gum. They waited for the family to pass before they rose from their seats and walked to their car for the trip to the cemetery.

The procession to the hallowed ground was short and it would not be long before Lynette would finally be laid to rest. The proof of her misdeeds would never again see the light of day.

The October afternoon was sunny and still, except for the sudden song of a whippoorwill in the distant woods, stabbing the silence and melting into it again. Some sumacs were reddening on the opposite hillside; and the adjoining meadow was a gently rolling green and brown sea guarded by cattails that grew at the edge of the millpond. The murmur of frogs that were accompanied by the aroma of mown hay lifted and drifted on any wandering breath of wind.

On the opposite side of the millpond, Cathy's eyes were drawn to the play of light and shadows upon its surface. The sun shone unrelentingly, until it would slowly sink toward the horizon, and she admired the cool green depths of the millpond beneath the overhanging trees. *He's in there!* She turned her eyes back toward Gigi, but said nothing and kept walking.

A path had been mown through the city of LaFayette's former citizenry, and Martin Stinson walked behind Lynette's casket in a well-tailored dark blue suit that would have made his mother proud. He assisted Charles who, despite his age, maneuvered well some of the uneven terrain. Lynette's grave was on the left side of Judge's in the family's burial plot, which lay under a large oak, and was enclosed by an ancient, crooked wrought-iron fence. Everyone took their places and waited for the beginning of the graveside service.

A mockingbird, balancing on a leaning slate headstone, burst into a gurgling laughter of song, not suitable for the occasion, and the oak dropped moving shadows back and forth on the group of men and women who stood watching, silently, that solemn merging of living into Life—of consciousness and knowledge and bitterness and spite, of human nature into Nature.

Cathy surmised that at his advanced age, even Charles, mourning and bewildered, felt an uplifting of humanity—the dignity, the mercy, and the graciousness of Death, emancipating fettered souls who had stumbled and struggled on this plane, to emerge into clear, clean spaciousness among the stars. She, however, found it difficult to fathom the ending of Lynette's mean and pitiful tumult, encompassed with all of its primitive emotions, which is so often all that anyone's individuality seems to be. *Such a sweet service*.

As Cathy stared at Lynette's casket, she thought of the sinking of this one iota of Life into the Universe being like the subsidence of a little whirling gust of wind which, for an instant, has caught up straws and dust and then drops into dead calm. In the realm of the Universe, Lynette's nine plus decades were little more than tiny ripples undulating across the vast waters of Existence, itself.

A variety of thoughts and emotions tumbled through her head, and she barely heard the minister's words of comfort. Her attention had been drawn to the afternoon sun, which she felt had undoubtedly captured the attention, veneration, and the worship of primitive races, or so she thought. *Nature depends absolutely on the presence and support of the Sun.* She astrologically considered the Sun to constitute the central Life Principle, of which Lynette was now a part, and would be aware of no more. The ability to control her mind had left her, and she thought, my mind has a mind of its own, and pursed her lips at the absurdity.

Cathy felt a sense of peace, not exactly human, but organic; perhaps, the kind that only comes where there is no grief. Lynette's friends and neighbors had felt it, too, Cathy reasoned, for as she, they stood watching, silently, unbelieving in their hearts that they, too, would some time go back into the sun and shade of the rolling Earth, where there is no grief, only curiosity and interest...and a sense of peace.

CHAPTER 29

Cathy tried to quell her mounting excitement as she and Gigi sat at the Sunrise Cafe. She couldn't believe that she was having coffee with not only Martin Clyde Stinson, but Charles Chambers, as well. Charles's aged hand trembled as he stirred his coffee, and Cathy tried to imagine his journey from the rough and tumble boy of yesteryear to the genteel gentleman who sat before her now. *I wonder if he knows how his father really felt about him.*

She had to exert her sheerest force of will to keep from telling them about the diary, for there were so many questions that she wanted to ask them. Framing these questions would be crucial, so as not to arouse their suspicions. If they had knowledge of the diary, the two would not rest until they were allowed to see it, and what they would find would forever change the perception of the woman they loved and thought they knew.

Cathy gingerly handed the photograph album across the table to Martin, and as he carefully opened it, Charles said, "My Lord, I haven't seen that old thing in years."

"Mother worked hard raising us," Martin began. "But, she always managed to keep food on the table and clothes on our backs through all those lean years."

"Yes," Charles added with exactness, "Lynette was good to all of us. I used to help her as much as I could, baking pies and cakes, doing the washing, and such. There's no telling what would have happened to me if she hadn't been there. I probably would have ended up with Aunt Mable." His hand still trembled as he stirred his coffee.

"Who is your mother?" Cathy addressed him for Gigi's benefit.

"Evelyn was my mother. Grandpa had three kids before he married Lynette: my mother, Aunt Mable, and Aunt Sara," he answered her questions as Martin thumbed through the pages and located Evelyn's picture. Cathy pretended not to know anything about her, but Gigi's interest was genuine.

"What about Mable? Did she marry?" she inquired, as she stirred her coffee.

"Aunt Mable never did marry," Charles replied.

"She was grown when I was born," Martin added, "So was her daughter, Ravanell."

"Ravanell? And who's her father?" Cathy asked in a lighthearted manner, and then noticed a look of embarrassment on Martin's face.

Charles alleviated the moment, "Well, you know back then, things was different than they are today. You know, young girls, they go out to have a good time and get into trouble. That's what happened to Aunt Mable, but Grandpa had influence in the community. Oh, yeah, there was gossip of course, but the story at the time was that Aunt Mable had met and married a soldier from New Jersey, and that he got killed in a construction accident after World's War I."

"Oh," Cathy nodded in understanding.

"But," he continued, "after we was all grown, I was talking to Ravanell...actually it was right after Aunt Mable's funeral, and she told me that Aunt Mable had once told her that her daddy was a fellow by the name of Fox. K.C. Fox, I think she said."

Cathy froze! *This just could not be!* She did not anticipate this news and hoped that the shock did not show on her face. This information, difficult for her to grasp, stung as much as a slap, and she hoped that her allegorically smarting face would not betray her. She groped for words, but none came to mind. Martin and Charles continued turning pages of the album and telling the family stories of the pages' inhabitants.

"Mable died more than twenty years ago. Cardiac arrest," Martin said, pointing out a picture of Mable and Hattie, picking up the lull in the conversation.

Cathy sipped her coffee and said, "Ravanell?"

"Ravanell passed on," Charles said, "just four days before her and Ned's fiftieth wedding anniversary. They had four children and lived in Florida."

"Where did you go, Charles?"

"Oh, after I graduated high school, I went to Emory in Atlanta," he chuckled, "That's where I met my wife. She was from Columbus, and after graduation and law school, we married and opened a law practice there."

"Your mother would've been so proud of you," Cathy said, "I'm sure Lynette was proud of both of you." She looked lovingly at Charles, again trying to envision how the boy she had come to know from the diary had grown into the gentle old man sitting across from her.

"Yes, she was," Martin offered, nodding his head, "Many's the time that I heard her comment to other people about how Charles had made something of himself."

"What about her family?" Cathy asked, trying to steer the conversation away from any connection to K.C. Fox.

"Well, there were three girls in her family," Charles said, sipping his coffee. "Her sisters, Aunt Maude, who was married to Uncle Thomas Shields, and then there was Aunt Baby."

"What happened to them?" Cathy asked, nonchalantly.

"Aunt Maude and Uncle Thomas lived in Chattanooga, up on Lookout Mountain," Martin added, "But, Aunt Baby, that was my Aunt Clydellen, she died. She ran a milk route from Rock Spring to LaFayette. In fact, she was killed in an accident just before I was born. Mama never got over it."

"I don't know why, but I was under the impression that your mother had a daughter," Cathy said, puzzled.

"Oh, she wanted a girl, all right. She was going to name her Mary Elizabeth, after a lady in town who was real good to her after Daddy died. And then, Aunt Baby got killed. Mama had quite a time of it. I was born on New Year's Eve, 1938, and was *not* the girl she had hoped for."

Cathy's eyes lit up. *So that's why the diary had ended so abruptly!* She smiled secretly in amusement. *Curiosity killed the cat, but satisfaction got him back!*

"When did she remarry?" Gigi guessed, nonchalantly.

Charles pursed his lips and rubbed his chin. He shook his head tenderly as he thought.

"I believe it was in 1948," Martin began.

"Yeah," Charles affirmed, "It was in '48. Lee Graham passed on in '42 and being the family lawyer, Oliver and Lynette had been friends for many years. It wasn't surprising to anyone when they finally married."

"Oliver was good to Mama and me," Martin added. "Oh, sure, people talked a bit, but not for long. Life was good for all of us."

"What happened to Oliver?" Cathy's curiosity could not be contained.

"He had a stroke in '78. Mama had him buried here next to Lee. She always knew that Lee was the love of his life and he'd want to be next to her."

"Your mother was a very kind and courageous woman," Cathy comforted.

"Yes," Martin said, "And now Mama is at rest next to Daddy."

Cathy was silent, as she had her suspicions about Lynette's lasting repose next to Judge. When Lynette's funeral arrangements had been made, the choice was one more that she had been denied, the circumstances having robbed her of yet another of life's choices. Now, maybe the dominoes of despair in Lynette's life would stop falling.

"Well," Charles said, emphatically, "When my time comes—."

There was a pause, and he sighed deeply. He seemed to be quietly choosing his words, perhaps slowed down a moment by other memories. Finally, he continued, "I don't want to be like Aunt Mable. She was never sick, until the end, of course. People always said that she was beautiful, and turned heads wherever she went. But, when she died, the way she looked...."

"She certainly didn't look like Mable," Martin agreed.

"Then, allow me my vanity," Charles implored, "I want to be remembered how I was; not how I am now. I don't want people looking down at me in a casket and saying things like how good I look, considering."

"Considering what?" Cathy was curious.

"Considering that when I was younger, the girls thought I was quite handsome, and age and sickness have destroyed what was once pleasing to so many people."

Gigi laughed and patted Charles's arm. "I don't think you have anything to worry about, Mr. Charles. You're still a looker. You're still turning heads!"

The group laughed, and Martin smiled at Charles's blush and said, "All right. You want a closed casket?"

Charles looked up at him, nodding, "Damned straight!"

CHAPTER 30

The late October afternoon was chilly as the small group stood on the sidewalk in front of the Sunrise Cafe. Standing in awkward silence, none of them seemed to know how they should end their conversation. A door opened behind them and, automatically, everyone stepped aside to let the exiting patrons pass.

It felt strange and absurd, that having just met Martin and Charles, Cathy felt so comfortable with them, and she found herself wanting them to stay. Maybe it was the end of this adventure, or maybe she was just being selfish, but she wanted more. Her time without Harry had been so consumed that she felt a high level of desperation at the prospect of no longer unraveling the riddle. The thrill of the chase, so to speak, had spurred her on from clue to clue, and she wondered how she would cope, now that the matter was laid to rest.

"I'll be coming back in about a month to settle Mama's affairs," Martin said, fumbling with the zipper on his smart brown jacket, which had replaced his suit coat after the funeral. Charles nodded.

"Well, call me when you get here, and maybe we can go out to dinner or something," Cathy said, "You've got my number."

Martin patted his pocket, "I've got it right here. That sounds fine. I can't tell you how nice it is to meet you and Gigi. You have no idea how much I appreciate you looking after Mama. I'm going to miss her so. Even though I wasn't with her, just knowing that she was in the world made it easier to get by day to day. I always had her to turn to."

Cathy winced and nodded, saying nothing. Gigi saved the moment by sticking out her hand to shake theirs and said, "It is a privilege to meet both of you, too."

Cathy surmised that she could get back to work on the chest. She hadn't told Martin and Charles about it, so maybe she could finish the work and surprise Martin with it...as a gift. *A poor exchange for his mother's life.*

Gigi and Cathy stood silently in the evening breeze as they watched Martin escort an elderly and ailing Charles to Martin's blue sedan. He carefully helped Charles into his seat and took great pains to see that his seat belt was buckled properly, much as Cathy thought that Lynette might have done when Charles had first come under her wing in 1931, had their roadsters been equipped with seat belts.

Even though advances in civilization and technology had made contemporary life easier for society, the elements of Nature remained unchanged. Winter gripped the towns and houses and the people, and with icy hands had threatened to choke the life-sustaining heat from their bodies. Summer greedily sapped the strength of the heartiest during the grueling heat waves of long days when the whole world seemed to be on fire. It took special people to withstand these elements; people with the strength of heart and the fortitude to outlast these hardships and to survive. And that's exactly what they had done. They had survived.

Martin threw up his hand to them as he got into his car, and Cathy felt somewhat affected by the gesture. She wanted to run up to the window and open the door and confess everything to him and to beg his forgiveness. But, solemnly she stood and watched them drive away, leaving LaFayette and a life that seemed commonplace eons ago.

When the tail lights of the car were out of sight, Gigi looked at Cathy inquisitively. "You all right, Cat?"

"Yeah, I'm fine," she answered, "Hey, do you care if we drive by the house one more time before we go back to Chattanooga?"

"Sure. Did you find what you were looking for?" Gigi asked, intuitively.

"I don't know," Cathy answered, thoughtfully, "but, I think so."

Cathy and Gigi sat in the car in front of Lynette's house. Stepping back in time, she could hear the click and whir of the blades of a lawn mower as Charles cut the grass, and she could see Mable and Hattie running in the front door, slamming it behind them, in their hurry to get ready for a night on the town. She thought of hot summer nights when Lynette, Charles, and Miss Myrtle would sit eating homemade ice cream on the front porch, and cool mornings when Baby would walk around to the back door singing her favorite song.

In her heart, Cathy held the secrets of Judge's demise at Lynette's hands, as well as K.C. Fox's, aided by Lynette's beloved Baby. She did not know when Lynette had planned Judge's death, or how long she had been poisoning him. There was no one whom she could ask.

She did know, however, when Lynette had reached the point where she could no longer cope with her situation, and had gently covered his face with his pillow until he capitulated and ceased to breathe. *Why had there been no one there to help her— or to stop her?* Only God knew the answers to those questions.

Cathy felt strangely sympathetic. K.C.'s death had not been planned, but had evidently been the culmination of his broken promises and Lynette's uncontrollable frustration and rage, coupled with the realization that he had only been using her. *How brave Lynette must have been, to be outwardly docile while she was screaming inside. Making such difficult decisions during extremely emotional times*. Cathy mused these points as she lightly puffed on her cigarette.

She felt a chill as cool air brushed her cheek, and her gaze was drawn to the street corner where she imagined, at one time, Hattie Winslow stood in the lamplight flirting with K.C. Fox while Lucile waited for him at home with her children. She knew these people, and had no idea how she had become so intimately involved with their lives and their secrets, yet she cared deeply for them. Before leaving, Cathy knew that she must go back to the cemetery for one last good-bye. Gigi was ready to go back to Chattanooga, but relented for Cathy's sake, and said that she would wait for her in the car.

A few leaves fell from a maple tree as Cathy entered the darkening cemetery. Across the meadow, the sun was setting beyond the millpond and shadows were beginning to gather in the twilight. She made her way carefully between the headstones and the shadows. This is it, she thought, this is the place. She quickly located the burial plot and stood before the newest grave, easily found due to the mountain of flowers which resembled a varicolored quilt. Everyone was gone now, and Lynette had been left with the cold and the quiet, and her eternal peace. Only Cathy shared this moment with her.

Cathy contemplated, with quiet understanding, all that had happened that day. Lost in thought, she saw herself standing before Lynette's open casket for the final viewing. *Let the dead bury the dead.* She could not remember when or where she had heard that, but the thought seemed to be appropriate as she had secretly slid the diary into the casket and had quickly tucked it underneath Lynette's blue dress. Now, standing over the grave, Cathy knew that Lynette could rest easily, having literally taken her secrets to the grave.

Solving the mystery of the diary had been her mission, her purpose, and she felt that half of the joy of discovery was sharing that which she had discovered. She could reveal it to no one, however, for whomever she told would probably require proof, and the proof was no longer available. *What kind of person can poison another and then, suffocate them for not dying fast enough? What kind of person can vent their rage by raising a shovel and bringing it crashing down on the skull of a person who doesn't even see it coming? What kind of person, covered by darkness, can totally dismember a body, pack it in milk cans, and then, dump it into a watery grave?* Maybe, she only thought she knew Lynette and Baby.

She was still not quite ready to leave LaFayette. As she gazed out toward the millpond, she tried to imagine how the roadway had been in 1938. The old cars slogging through the mud made ruts in her mind as she imagined the sheets of rain in the wind; and the fervor that was caused in the town when, thanks to President Roosevelt and the CCC, the dirt road had been transformed into a two-lane blacktopped highway. Her mind's eye cast toward an Orenduff Dairy milk truck as it stopped at Trammel's Mill to make "deliveries."

Her thoughts turned to Mr. Mack and his cousin, Thad, who had been incarcerated for a year for the manufacture of moonshine, when their only infractions had been being born poor and black and living in a Southern town. Cathy wondered if Lynette had ever known that her father had traded her to Judge in order to stay out of jail, and found herself wondering how Clyde had lived with himself all those years, having sold his daughter. Marcus Trammel had been no fool. It wasn't by accident that he had been seeing Mable, on the side, of course.

To the right of Lynette's grave, she saw Judge's, and buried to her left were her beloved Sammie and Markie, gone these many years, now Angels in Heaven. She imagined her eyes were playing tricks on her, or maybe it was the twilight. Lynette lay at the foot of Judge's grave, crying her heart out for her beloved K.C., and her sorrow and her remorse, profound. Now, throughout the cemetery, the spirits were actively going about their business, the ones who had gone on before now owning the land. Hattie Winslow seemed to stroll at her leisure, and Miss Mary Lizzie smiled demurely and nodded her head knowingly.

A young woman meandered and cooed, caressing a baby in her arms, and Cathy knew her to be Georgia Turner with a lavender silk scarf concealing the rope burn around her neck. She could see Mable running to

Hattie, the two school chums reunited after years of estrangement, picking up where they had left off, in frolicking and felicity. The gadabouts were followed by Helen and William...and then, there was Lucile, solemn and broken, older than her years, who had never remarried after K.C.'s disappearance and who had, as folks told it, died of a broken heart at the age of thirty-nine.

The cemetery seemed to be filled with members of the community, long forgotten, who had come to greet Lynette. Their smiles were genuine and their sorrows had faded. Oliver and Lee, together in their timeless love, and Judge, stoic and hard, as in his former life, Mrs. Rhyne, Tommy and Emily, Ravanell and Ned, Brother Story, and on and on.

A silhouette caught her eye. A lone, lanky figure stood at the edge of the millpond, and Cathy knew that it was none other than K.C. Fox, himself, unable to enter the cemetery, unable to leave the millpond; his destiny uncertain. His life of seducing and discarding women as easily as he would discard a pair of old shoes had finally caught up with him. Selfishly, satiating his desires had created actions that had affected the lives of so many people, totally unaware of one another. He was a spider, entangling flies in his sticky web, feasting on them before leaving their hollowed shells wrapped in strands that connected them to other hollowed shells. Cathy wondered if Lynette had found it in her heart to forgive him.

The twilight was magical and elegant and comforting. She heard sweet familiar strains and turned to see Baby lumbering up a slope, coming to greet her sister, singing, "Go tell Aunt Rhody, go tell Aunt Rhody, go tell Aunt Rhody, the old gray goose is dead."

Lynette turned and stared up at Cathy, and when she fathomed the forgiveness on the dead woman's face, Cathy's bitter helplessness burst forth in tears and anguish that were directed nowhere. *How can she ever forgive me?*! But, Lynette's forgiveness was genuine and her loving smile, comforting.

Baby's voice transcended the decades, clear and melodious, as Cathy walked to her car in the evening shadows. This whole episode had started when she had discovered Lynette's diary of despair. *Why would she have written such happenings, and why would she have kept them all of these years? Such damning evidence could have destroyed her and her family, and keeping it could only have been a threat. Maybe, she really wanted to get caught.*

Then, a fresh idea occurred to her; something that she had not done. Perhaps, the time had come to stop living in the past. Perhaps, she would go back to school and resume her nursing education and career, and reenter the world of the living. The end of the year was approaching, and Cathy mulled over the thought of writing a diary of her own next year—a diary of hope.

She paused at the cemetery gate and turned to see Baby and a young Lynette in a sisterly embrace, and she knew that Lynette was truly in Heaven now. Suddenly, she thought of Harry...and she smiled.

The End

About Thornton Parsons

Born in Jacksonville, Florida, Thornton Parsons resides in the beautiful Tennessee Valley where she taught high school English in Chattanooga. She is a weekly columnist for *LS NewsGroup* and when she's not writing, she spends her time travelling and conducting research. The author believes in the creed: "Every life should have nine cats."

Made in the USA
Monee, IL
10 January 2024

51533894R00154